CHIKELUE OKOYE

OBODOM

SCRIPTOR HOUSE
The Epitome of Greatness

Scriptor House LLC
2810 N Church St Wilmington, Delaware, 19802
www.scriptorhouse.com
Phone: +1302-205-2043

Paperback ISBN: 979-8-88692-178-6
eBook ISBN: 979-8-88692-179-3

This book is dedicated first and foremost to the almighty God that granted me the enablement. I also dedicate it to my beautiful wife, **Ifeoma** *and wonderful children,* **Chisom, Ndochukwu, Chimamaka, Kachimsicho,** *and* **Odilimmma**. *I love you all.*

ONE

• •

The night was breaking into morning and the entire area will soon wake up to its hustle and bustle. All her belongings were packed and hidden away from the glare of the public. She wobbled as she moved away from under the fly-over that had become her home. It was becoming increasing difficult for her to walk. The luxury of a bath was forgotten. It was the 'harmattan' weather, the country's version of winter. As has become the case recently the weather was extremely cold. She wore all her clothes but there was still no succour from the cold.

"When will all these mysterious ill feeling end?" She wondered. In any case, it was no longer mysterious to her. She had understood that she was pregnant. At thirteen she had to fend for her living as well as nurture her pregnancy. It was not her choice or she would not have been pregnant. The awe of the day it had all started kept replaying through her mind. It was difficult for her not to remember.

She was hawking her wares on the street disturbed that she had not made good sales for the day. A man requested of her to follow him to his house which was not far for him to conveniently keep the items in his house afterwards. He wanted to buy all that she had and even requested her to bring him more supplies the next day. Happily she followed him. She never knew of his accomplice who suddenly emerged behind her and shoved her into an uncompleted building, clamping his palm over her mouth. These men collected the money she had realized, raped and beat her up. She rushed home in tears to narrate her ordeal knowing nothing else to do. Her guardian was uncaring whatever happened to her. She was rather aghast that she came back with empty tray without the wares or money. After giving her the beating of her life she warned her sternly to go and not to come back home again without the money. That instance she left marked the onset of her current life's-script.

"Don't come back if you fail to get the money for the items you sold. I do not want you back except it is to bring the money." Her guardian warned throwing a bag containing her few belongings at her. She never ever got the money and was so horrified that she never went back. That would not have been much of a problem if she had not become pregnant. She had been hawking from when she was 7 years old. This has equipped her with good knowledge of the locality. It had

1

taken her to the nooks and crannies of the city. It was not enough however to equip her with the knowledge of the inherent dangers neither did it equip her on how to avert them. For all intents and purposes, she had ceased caring.

There was no doubt anymore about her being pregnant. There was equally no doubt in her mind that a lot is happening within her. "Whatever am I going to do? What am I supposed to do?" The questions were many but no answers. She was however determined and had resolved to overcome each second and live on.

In blissful expectations she waited for the rising of the morning sun. She was always thankful whenever she feels the soothing warmth that it gives her. It strengthens her for the day. She also loved the occasional conventional rains that follow those very hot and sunny afternoons. On such occasions of rainfall, the burden of sourcing water to bath was taken care of. She normally sought secluded locations to remove her clothing to the barest minimum without going completely naked. Her tired frame can equally not wait for the dusk that bids the daily bustle and hustle bye. For her, life simply goes on. All that it has to offer were welcome with joy and anticipation. She has learnt that the best way to get on in life was to do the things she wanted to do promptly enough and cherish the ones she was not capable of changing.

"When I deliver my baby, I will have a family of my own. I will have a companion and some one of my own to love and cherish." The thought of having a baby pleased her and she clung on to that hope and expectation to give living a meaning. Her mind drifted to the things she had seen nursing mothers do. There were worries in her mind too. However, she held onto the thoughts that made her happy rather than the ones that frightened her.

The day will come and go. My baby must be born. I will assist and love my baby. I will be there for him to grow into an eminent adult. 'I will definitely be there', she affirmed. Will my baby be boy or girl? What will my baby look like? What will his future be? The thoughts and questions kept coming. They were endless as they were unceasing. She knew however that time will tell.

The awaited time eventually came. She could not understand the way she felt. "I am definitely going mad" she worried. The pain was more than she could bear. Her abdomen was contracting as if some strange forces wanted to squeeze the baby inside her belly to death. "Am I dying? What is really happening to me?"

Then suddenly a mixture of blood and water gushed out from between her legs which were strange to her. There was never any urge for her to urinate. "I am definitely dying," she started wailing and shouting not knowing exactly what to do.

Suddenly she found herself in the mist of some ladies. It got her all the more scared. "What is happening to me?" she managed to ask one of the ladies.

Instead of an answer, the lady looked at her patronizingly without altering a word. She has her own worries, too. The tears came naturally as she wondered 'she is only a child, will she be able to go through this?'

With the assistance of the rest, she took her to a nearby hospital. Being a nurse, she realized that the young girl's medical need was going to be complex. 'Will she survive it?' She equally wondered. 'It is only time that will tell,' she concluded. Realizing the young girl was waiting for an answer, "your baby is coming," she answered trying to hide her worries with a smile.

She needed to know quite a lot from her. Who is she? Where is she living? There was no need asking of a husband. She could not have been married at that age. It dawned on her that the girl must have been sexually violated.

Somehow she resolved to get as much information from her as possible. Much of this information will be required in the hospital.

"I am Geraldine James. Please tell me who you are."

"Juliana Agozie," She simply replied.

"Where do you live?" She persisted.

"I do not have a home," she answered and in between sobs, told as much of her story as she could.

The pains came very strong again as they arrived the hospital. She stopped talking. Her breaths were coming in gasps.

"Geraldine immediately identified herself even as she requested for emergency attention to the girl. Her medical experience alerted her to the danger the girl's life was confronted with. Her baby's situation was no better. It will be a miracle for her to deliver normally. She was absolutely too young and her organs still too tender for the ordeal of child bearing. She equally needed no telling that

Juliana never had any form of medical attention from the time of conception till then. She can only hope for the best, that both her and her child survives.

'Dear Good Lord, please grant her the enablement to survive this' she prayed silently.

Finally, she was moved into the delivery ward. There was no time to take any records. She was too weak to talk. The only thing she could afford to do was to look up to Geraldine. There were a lot she wanted to tell her.

She was an angel. She wanted to simply tell her thank you. All that she could do was to keep mopping at her. It was much of a luxury to expect someone as kind in her life anymore. This is especially judging from her life experience. Her mind reflected on how she had left home.

'If only she had been my guardian, I would not have gone through all these' she reminisced bitterly.

"Are you going to leave me?" She asked instead. "Please don't ever leave me. Don't ever send me away. There is nowhere to go. I don't want my baby to live like me. I don't want anyone to harm him or beat him. He is 'Obodom'- my community, my life, my friend. Help me protect him."

Managing to hold her tears, "I am here for you," she assured her.

It was the last discussion they had before she lost consciousness. It was equally the last discussion they will ever have. She was delivered of a boy but could not make it herself she lived no more. Geraldine kept looking at the boy in her hand. A million things went through her mind.

Whatever am I going to do? The irony of life dawned on her. Her marriage had crumbled because she had no child.

'Here am I with Juliana's baby.' She thought sadly as she remembered their last discussion before her death.

'Why is the world so? Why has humans made life so complex that the fun of living is gone? Is the world intended to be so or is it the making of mankind. There is so much wickedness in life. What will be the future of Obodom? She had decided there and then that his name will be 'Obodom'. Will I be able to guarantee the future wanted for him by his late mother?'

Amidst all these wonders and worries she finally made up her mind.

'Whatever it will take me or cost me I will take care of you. I will cherish and love you like my own son for that is precisely what you have become. I will train and nurture you to manhood. You will rule your world. I swear that as long as there is God, I will take care of you. You will rise from orphan to leadership. You will move this world positively. I swear. Yes, I swear.'

Her resolve was so intense and so deep that she started shivering as her body was covered with goose pimple.

TWO

It was 31ˢᵗ day of March and Obodom Agozie had just turned 18years old. There must be something special about this day. The day meant so much to him. It could be called the day of unveiling. He was very apprehensive and jittery. A lot will be unveiled today. He was not just growing into manhood but a lot of mysteries that have deluded him from childhood will be revealed. In answer to some questions he had often been told to wait for this 'great story'. When he requested that he be told the great story, the mother had assuredly and pleasantly told him to wait until he was 18 years old. It had been as if his 18ᵗʰ birthday will never come. At last the day has come.

'There is no more waiting. The time has finally come.' He thought, a little frightened and jittery. Any story that he had to wait until he was 18 must indeed be a great story.

It was not just him that the day meant so much to. Geraldine James has become sick all on the account of the same day. There were so much that traversed her mind at the moment. Beyond that day there will be great changes no doubt. It was not the anticipated changes that mattered to her. The nature of the change was the issue. She regretted being the one to tell him.

A look at his table clock jolted him off his bed. It was 7:30am and he was still in his bed. The family normally wake by 5am. Surprising too, his mother has not woken up either. He felt a bit hurt that she has not wished him happy birthday.

'That is quite unlike mom.' He thought. He became afraid that something may have gone wrong and made for her room in haste.

"Mom, Mom," he called as he rushed into her room.

She was shivering and in tears when he entered.

"Mom, it is my birthday and you are weeping, what has gone wrong?"

She clasped unto him in a great emotional throb and started crying.

"Pardon me my son, I will tell you the story I promised you today. I am so scared of what will happen after.

"Please sit down there is no need to wait anymore.

6

"You once asked me why the two of us have different surnames quite unlike what obtains between other mothers and their children. I believe you still remember. It was a question I could not answer you then but today I have to explain everything to you - I am not your biological mother. I have to wait until you are grown up to let you know. Yes, I could have decided not to tell you by letting you bear my surname. That would have been the most natural thing to do. There would not have been any reason to explain anything at all in the first place. That would have hidden the entire story.

"I decided against that. It will amount to disservice to your mother. I would have failed on the charge she gave me before your birth. I have sworn a solemn oat to myself to do all that can be done in respect of your great mother. She was so young but a great personality. She is a wonderful girl you have every reason to be proud of.

"Many people will not agree with me that she is great. That is only because a lot of us are corrupt in values. Right things become right only as much as the party involved is prominent or wealthy. The non-prominent and the down trodden members of the society are nonentities and charlatans by such people's standard. By their standards heroes and heroines are only found among the rich and the affluent. The real heroes that withstand the evil tempest and hurricane of the effect of maladministration, destroyed environment, greed and corruption in high places, lack of infrastructure and basic needs of life to become the champions and pictures of what is ideal are the un song of the society. You should be proud of your mother.

"She is my heroine. She is but a child, but that qualified her better as my heroine.

"She was driven by a wicked guardian that took advantage of her having a poor background. A woman that took advantage of a child that cannot fend for herself. Rather than assist her to overcome the challenges of life, she threw her to the dangers of the society. Her only concern was that she should hawk wares and return the proceeds to her. She may have been poor, but this did not and would not have made right for her to subject the little girl to child labour. She never bordered about the dangers she was exposed to. Your mother, my heroine faced the dangers of the enterprise until she was assaulted, raped and the money from her sales snatched.

7

"The only regret of her guardian was the money that was snatched from her. She sent her out to the street with her few belongings never to come back except she has her money. She became pregnant not knowing what pregnancy was and what it entails. She has such a passionate heart that she did not waste useful time thinking of her ordeal or guardian. She focused rather on her coming baby. The nine months period was without any medical assistance or aid. She fought the battle all alone. She has so much strength and courage. Her love for her yet to be born baby was so great. She forgave her assailants and did the noble thing by dedicating all her love to her yet to be born baby"

She paused to collect a parcel that was by her bedside.

"I have always given you gifts for your birthdays. I will do same today only that today's gift is particularly unique and significant. I hope, however that it will become your turning point to greatness which is the wish of your mother. I am wishing that the importance of all these will not be lost on you. The day has come that you have to take your decisions and make your choices. I will only be your guide and adviser if I have your permission.

"There is no need mentioning that I will bear your educational and upkeep expenses until you become employed.

"The things you see in this parcel have special meaning to me. I earnestly hope they will mean same or even more to you." She said as she opened the parcel.

There were three laminated photographs, a birth registration certificate of Obodom Agozie who was born 31st March, a death registration certificate of Juliana Agozie who died 31st March, a bank passbook in the name of Obodom Agozie, and gold coloured necklace with a cross pendant.

"Obodom Agozie, today I make it clear to you that I am only your guardian and not your mother. In the time past I have wanted a baby of my own. My not having one broke my marriage. I lived in bitterness ever since. My meeting your mother and consequently you changed all that. I see motherhood differently now. Being a parent means a different thing to me now. Parenthood is the charge divinely given to men and women to look around to see those children requiring their support to provide it. It is not a possession or ownership. Possessiveness as preferring one's personal biological children is borne out of selfishness and that is the bane of the society.

"For this reason, I decided not to give you my own surname. Apart from letting down your mother it would have been nothing other than child theft on my path. If I have done that perhaps you would have been living in ignorance. Your affection towards me would have been treacherously obtained. It would not have given you the impetus to change the society in which you find yourself for the better.

"Always remember the words of your mother. It was her last before you were born – 'Please don't ever leave me. Don't ever send me away. There is nowhere to go. I don't want my baby to live like me. I don't want anyone to harm him or beat him. He is 'Obodom'- my community, my life, my friend. Help me protect him.'

"Your mother was poor but what she bequeathed to you is so great. The bank passbook is of your account. I opened it with part of the money I found in her belonging. The balance portion of the money was used to open an investment account to facilitate investing in mutual funds and bonds for you. The value of your stock portfolio and bank account currently will surprise you tremendously. Now that you are 18, the management and running of both will be reverted to you.

"The birth and death certificates belong to you. One of the three photographs was her picture when maybe she was 9 years; one is you as a baby of 3 months, while the other is your mother as at her death. The gold coloured necklace with cross pendant is cheap in cost but very expensive in value. It meant so much to her. She held on it as if her life depended on it when she was in labour. She was still holding it when she had her last breadth. I know she must have been praying that God should keep her alive to love, train and bring you up."

He got up from where he was seated. His hands were shaky as he picked up the photograph. First he beheld his real mother. The picture came alive in his mind as he looked at it so intently. It was her picture as a corpse. She was really a baby. The look on her face was so peaceful. Without being told, he knew why. She was so content to bid this wicked world bye after she had handed her only treasure Obodom – me into the hands of my current mother.

Suddenly, tears sprout out from his eyes and dripped down his cheeks. It was difficult for him to interpret his feelings. A lot was going through his mind at that moment. He was angry at his late mother's guardian for her wickedness and heartlessness. He was angry at the men that could take advantage of thirteen years

9

old, robbing her of both her money and virginity. He was angry at the society that offered no protection for the less privileged. Yes he was extremely angry at the society where no voice is raised against the enslavement of children in child labour.

Taking the three pictures, he walked quietly out of the room. He needed to be on his own.

'What kind of society is it where there is no protection for the weak, the poor and the under privileged? Where a thirteen years girl will bear pregnancy for 9 months and no agency cared.'

He felt such a deep love for her. How he wished she was still alive. How he wished she was there so that he would tell her how much he loved her.

He started crying. It was difficult not to.

'How on earth can such happen? Could somebody not have done anything about it? What is the government for if there is no protection for someone like my mother? Is there justice at all for the poor? If there is, his late mother's guardian and those that rapped her would all have been thrown into jail. He felt so angry realizing that chances are that they were all still living freely in the society and perhaps committing more atrocities. His late mother's guardian will continue in her use of child labour of innocent young children of the poor. Those riffraff too will be wherever they choose assaulting and rapping children and no one or agency raises a hand against them.'

One of the pictures fell from his hands. As he bent to pick it his eyes fell on childish attempt at drawing a baby and a scribbling on the back –'baby.' It was obvious to him that his biological mother did that. He felt so deeply touched that in her deprivation, she still can afford so much love.

Suddenly, he reflected on his philanthropic mother. She was the only person that took it upon herself to assist his biological mother and himself. His anger at the society diminished. He would be unfair to rule every member of the society guilty. If they were all guilty of heartlessness he would not have been alive today. He had actually been unfair to her.

Getting back to her room he found her still sobbing.

"Mom," he called passionately.

"Please stop crying. I am confused and angry at what happened but I still realize how wonderful a person you are. I love you so much mom. You are not just a mother to me. You are indeed everything to me."

They clung to one another as they continued to sob. It was soothing and relieving to cry at that time. It was as soothing to Geraldine to realize that Obodom's love for her has not changed. It was also soothing to him realizing that she was so humane and kind to render a helping hand to a helpless poor girl and to take it upon herself the task of bringing up another's child as hers.

As Obodom reflected on all the things that happened on his 18th birthday, he suddenly felt older than his age. He was mostly in thought there after wondering what to do. Something must be done to correct the anomalies of the society. What his mother went through will not be in vain. Other children must not be allowed to go through the same in their lives. The society must do what has to be done to ensure it must not happen again. How the desired changes can be achieved, he does not know.

The same resolve that made his foster mother to passionately take him as her own child came over him. His biological mother perhaps is spiritually alive influencing people around her to involuntarily fight her course.

"Mom is there anything that can be done to ensure the kind of thing that happened to mother will not repeat again, I mean never happen again?"

"A lot can be done. However, I want you to realize that it is an enormous task. It is a duty that one may not be able to accomplish in a life time. The most important thing, my son, is to be doing something about it no matter how small. No matter how small the effort may seem, believe me it will go a long way in solving the overall problem."

There was that sudden realization of being a lucky orphan. 'What would have become of me if my foster mother was not there? Would I be alive in the first place? If I am lucky to be alive, perhaps I will have been in an orphanage and who knows if I will remain alive to be eighteen.' It was then, he made up his mind. First, he wanted to come to terms with what being an orphan entails.

'I will visit one orphanage a week, study and read as much about it as I can. I will endeavour to know about the under privileged in the society. Those that do not have people to defend them have to be defended. Those that do not have someone to speak on their behalf must be spoken for. They are the litmus of measurement of the wellbeing of the society. The nation cannot be right if things are wrong with them. Every society or nation's strength is limited by the weakest in the polity. I must fight to strengthen the weak of this nation. I shall do everything within my powers and ability to fight the cause of the ordinary man, woman, boy or girl of the society. I commit myself to fight for the downtrodden. I offer myself to be spokesperson and advocate God helping me,' he resolved.

THREE

• •

It was not imposed on him by any one. If what happened to his biological mother escaped the attention of everyone except that of his foster mother, there could be much more happening that no one was doing anything about. Perhaps worst things could have or are happening that no one was doing anything about. It was therefore natural for him to adopt such self-imposed fact findings that have taken him about 10 years then. There were different categories of deprivations and needs he have come to be aware of. They were much more than he ever imagined. Things were all becoming clearer to him every passing day. Understanding things as they were was not actually his worry. What capacity he had to make an impact was his worry. How was he going to tackle the problems – problems of child abuse, no societal support for the elderly and the indigent members of the society that cannot meet their basic need of accommodation, feeding and clothing?

A particular encounter really disturbed him. The encounter had a great impact on him. He met this young boy of about four years of age playing with a mad lady. Perhaps worst would have been his own case if his foster mother had not salvaged the situation. He will never cease to be grateful and appreciative that she rescued him from what would have amounted to death or complete abandonment in life as a child.

"Come," he called on him. "What are you doing there? You had better leave that lady alone and go home before she injures you." He was referring to the mad lady who he estimated to be about 20 or 21 years old.

It was not long after that he realized that the lady may be mad but she was the mother of the boy. No one knew who the father was other than the suspicions that a guard in a nearby departmental store could have been responsible for her pregnancy. The lady went through the 9 months of pregnancy without antenatal care. She has equally escaped the notice of the welfare agencies that have better ideas on how the yearly financial vote made for their agency was to be used other than wasting it on a pregnant mad lady or her likes in the society.

"What is your name?" he tried finding out.

"I don't know" was his sincere response.

How will he be aware that people bear names? How will he know what the norms of the society are when the only guide and guardian he had was a mad mother? A mad lady that was ideal enough for a sane man to impregnate but the duty of care as expected of him, he was very eager to abandon. For the irresponsibility of a man like him, a boy was brought into the world to suffer.

'He will never suffer.' He vowed. 'For the sake of my late mother and my foster mother, you will live to be great. The memory of your childhood will be an inspiration to the entire Nation and the world. I will ensure that you will have whatever comfort any child is entitled to. I will stake my life and resources to make you a great man. Yes, a man that will be of substance, a responsible virtuous man that work for the liberation of his society from injustices of the oppressors.

'I swear, your mother may be mad; your father may not be known like mine – you will positively affect your world and your nation. You will leave your footsteps on the annals of history. The world will celebrate you as one of the greatest men that will ever live. You will wake this Nation from its slumber to become not only the giant of Africa, but the mover of the world. I swear that with the enablement and by the power of the almighty God, you will move your world. Through you God will heal this Nation.'

He was not in doubt that the task he had taken upon himself was great. He was also fully aware that accomplishing it was going to be daunting and difficult.

'It must be done', he enthused himself.

'Things must not be allowed to continue this way. I cannot allow things to continue to go wrong. It is the collective inaction of people that enables the undesired to continue to thrive.

'If there is that collective will to challenge and change things that are wrong in the society; if there are that collective resolve to say 'No to impunity', civility will become the order of the day.'

He cannot afford to let this boy or people like him down. It was difficult to even imagine failing his late mother.

He touched his chest to feel the cross pendant that had never left his neck since 10 years ago when he heard about his mother. It has become like a divine connection between him and his late mother. It was a source of inspiration, courage and determination in challenging situations and times like this.

'I have to find a way to assist this boy and his young but mad mother.' He was determined.

First of his task was to consult a lawyer to ensure that he would not go against the law. He equally sought for ways to provide medical attention to both the boy and the mother.

"If it will not go against the law, I will like to be the boy's guardian to ensure I will be able to give him the best I can." He confided in the legal practitioner. "I will like him to be under the comfort of my guidance and care. Please put in all your effort to legally make it possible.

"The boy can return to the mother when she becomes alright and is rehabilitated. I will not insist on any adoption. I only want to be the boy's benefactor. I want him not to lack any thing that I can afford. Please help me. Do consider this matter as of utmost importance to me. You may not understand but it means a lot to me."

He reflected on what happened during his eighteenth birthday - such life turning occurrence to a very great extent educated him on some of the challenges of life.

'Can there be joy in the company of the sorrowful? Can there be adequacy in the company of the deprived? Can there be fulfilment in the company of the hopeless?'

"There can never be any of these accomplishments when it does not apply to all," He replied loudly to the pondering of his mind.

"God help me. Please, do help me God. Help me to fulfil my heart desire to be a shoulder for the deprived to lean on. Help me to completely eradicate the ills of my nation that had deprived a greater majority of the citizens the benefit of the great blessings you have bestowed on this country."

The mad lady was admitted into the psychiatric hospital for treatment. A photograph of her was placed on the national papers and on the television in an effort to make proper identification of her.

Barrister Ahmed Nasser, the lawyer working out things for Obodom called to see him. He was anxious on the development of things. He never imagined it was going to take such a long time to have things worked out. While the state did not object to Obodom financially taking care of things, it was explained that there was need to serve some legal notices if things were to be done right.

He was willing to wait for things to be done right. He recalled his foster mother's assertion about parenthood

'Parenthood is the charge divinely given to men and women to look around to see those children requiring their support to provide it. It is not a possession thing. Possessiveness as preferring one's personal biological children is borne out of selfishness and that is the bane of the society'

It dawned on him the correctness of her philosophy in saying so.

'I will do my best.' He concluded as he welcomed Barrister Ahmed Nasser.

"Ahmed, what news do you bring me?" He asked.

"There is a new development a minor issue but which I realize will make you happy to handle.

"As the legal papers were being prepared for your ward if you permit my stating it as such, I realized that no name has ever been mentioned of him. This meant the boy has no name of his own. There is the need none the less for him to have name so that the legal documentation will at the least be tied to an identifiable legal entity.

"I know that it will amount a lot to you to have the privilege of naming him. In order that it happens I had serious engagements at the Child welfare board and there was no objection to that. So what name do you want to give him?"

He looked up at the lawyer, eyes clouded with tears. At that instance a lot went through his mind.

'If you have known me,' he thought of his companion, 'you would have known that it was nothing but divine providence that ensured I am alive. I was not in any way better than him.

'If not for the intervention of my foster mother, I wouldn't have had this God given opportunity to be of service to mankind.' He could not and did not tell him anything. It was however very sobering to find himself in such a situation. Probably, he will tell him later.

"I thank you Barrister Ahmed for the wonderful job you are doing. God will greatly reward you. I will request for a day to think very well. I will like to give him a befitting name. However, regarding his surname, I will want us to wait until the conclusion of the trace of the mother's identity. If there must be one, I will suggest his surname be Nigeria. I have this pre monition that he will play a significant role in the history of this nation. Whatever is making me to think and feel as I do, I cannot tell.

"I will not like to treat his mother so disrespectfully as to impose a surname on him different from hers if matters can be helped."

When and immediately Barrister Nasser Ahmed left him, his head was flooded with thousands of thoughts. He required not just time but also a calm and serene environment. Gently and thoughtfully, he paced to the garden in the rear of their building. The gentle breeze of the evening was quite welcome by his mood. He stretched himself on the lawn still thinking. The sound of flow of the stream in the back ground with the punctuating melody of the birds temporarily took his mind off his immediate concerns.

'Life is good,' he reflected, wondering why everyone can't be happy.

'There is simply enough of life's comfort for everyone,' he thought further as he dozed off into a thoughtful sleep.

He woke up remembering the discussion he once had with a friend bordering on a Benin name, 'Osayiwmense.' The discussion that day was on Nigerians giving their children names based on the meaning they want to portend in the family or the person's life. They were at this instance thrilled with the meaning of this Benin name.

A family have been facing series of ordeals – pre mature accidental deaths, ladies dying during child birth, mysterious deaths and the rest like. There was this courageous member of this family who not unmindful of these happenings affirmed when the wife was in labour.

'My wife you will deliver in peace by the name of God. You and our baby will be hale and hearty whatever the devil and his evil agents are thinking and planning. The child will not lack any thing. God will pave his way in life. People will look at him and confess that he is God's perfect creation. Here and now awaiting the traditional naming ceremony day, I state your name that it will be **Osayiwmense.'**

The name depicted the meaning of the man's assertions.

Obodom's search for a name for his ward was immediately decided.

'His name will be **Osayiwmense.** If he must be given a surname, then he must be **Osayiwmense Nigeria**.'

There was no doubt in his mind that Nigeria is potentially a great nation. A nation very much endowed in material and natural resources, the beautiful vegetation, the great natural tourist sites, solid mineral resources that dots almost all the states of the federation, the petroleum resources, the fertile grounds, the aquatic resources and its endowments, the diversity and creativity of its citizens.

'Osayiwmense, his generation and the ones after him will live and will enjoy the good of Nigeria. They will live in an era other nations will call, take and know Nigeria to be great' He was very confident of what he felt and thought of the future of the country. He cannot explain it but felt his intuition was right.

He has not stopped wondering, 'why do so many Nigerians fail to see the great endowment of the nation? Why has so many been eaten up with such despicable thoughts and believes about the nation even when the country is in itself a lot better than other nations of the world. Most Nigerians have their minds so polluted by the things they have been told or witnessed over the years that they no longer give Nigeria any chance of succeeding. They sing the same song alongside foreigners who in the first instance cared less about the country's survival.

'This must be stopped. A new order must emerge. The shackles of spiritual and mental slavery will be broken. Things have to change for the better. A new era has to be conceived. The greatest country not only in Africa but in the world is currently moving to the centre stage of world events. The members and partakers of the new order are emerging.

'They are going to be those that will actually arise whenever the Nigeria's call is made. They will and are going to serve their father land with all passion and devotion as has never been known before. The love for the nation will constantly glow in their hearts and mind. They will march the nation to the realization of its greatest potential. They will make the entire world and indeed most Nigerian's wonder what hid all these greatness earlier on that no one realized it.

'These people are indeed the true soldiers of the land. They are the true priests and religious leaders of the land. They are those that call on their Gods constantly to heal the wounds of the land. They also ceaselessly thank their Gods for the enormous blessings that the nation is endowed with.

'These are the men that have faith in the land. Their faith is so unadulterated and also does not waver even as their love is strong.

'These are the real compatriots that have sworn for the good of the land. These are the real compatriots that have sworn on oat to stand for, fight for and do all for the good of the land.

'They are the real leaders of the land. They are actually the ones working so hard to ensure that the gains of the works and labours of the nation's fallen heroes, the un celebrated great men and women that laid their lives for the liberation of the greatest nation of the world from the conspiracy of destruction being plotted by some nations that do not want a nation greater than theirs to emerge.

'These are the real leaders, though they did not go with the political title of 'President; Prime Minister; Governor' and the rest of such political leadership positions.

'The time has come when your service to the land is recognized and celebrated in actually making the nation of your dream to emerge.

'I swear this day to believe in what you believe in; stand for that that you stood for; live for that that you live for and eventually die for that that you died for – the greatest nation of the world'

FOUR

• •

He felt some sense of relief having decided on what he would do. There was no doubt in his mind that Nigeria is bound to be great. Her greatness however, can only be achieved by the citizens themselves. He was equally certain that there are quite an appreciable number of persons that do not like the way things are going on in the country. He will identify with such persons. If only they identify themselves and come together the change that is desired is achievable.

Things were unveiling at a great speed that made him realize how shallow his awareness of the problems of the country was. He was at a petrol station, dully queued like most others for petrol to be dispensed to his vehicle. There was the usual disgruntlement about such an experience in a country that the main stay of its economy is petroleum.

'Is it not dumbfounding that Nigerians queue to purchase fuel' complained one.

'We are indeed lucky that it is available these days. Have you forgotten the days that you can hardly get it to buy' commented another.

'There is actually great gains in democracy' chipped in yet another.

Obodom was filled with thought hearing all these discussions. People are thankful for the improvement that has come to be. Things have become so bad in the past that non-performance is the order of the day. Every minor improvement therefore is greatly celebrated.

He was appreciative of the positive mental attitude of some Nigerians. It had always been so painful whenever he encountered those that have given up on the country. To such persons nothing good will ever come out of Nigeria. However, he still understood very well why they felt so. Situations in the country have dealt such painful blows to them. None will want to go through the heart throbbing experience of going through failed and disappointed expectations.

'Are the perceived anomalies not the hind side of the unfulfilled beauties of the Land?

'Would people have been disappointed if it was not possible to turn things around for the better?

'Would Nigeria not be the greatest nation in the world if apart from having citizens of positive mental attitude towards their country she has also citizens who are not just willing to dream of the beauties of the land but also creators that manifest such dreams in realities?

'Will any improvement occur when nobody is doing anything?

'Can anything manifest out of nothing?

'Can there be harvesting without planting?

'When will the cultivation commence?

'Where are the farmers?

'Will any farmer leave his farm to go cultivating another's realizing that the harvest is not his?

'Why should we be content in admiring the flourishing farm of others? Do we see the flourishing farm and are unaware that it took the labour of the farmer who cultivated, nurtured and weeded it to make it so?

He was dazed in thought and oblivious of his environment. He was drawn back to consciousness hearing a hoarse voice besides him.

"Bros, how far? You enter town? You no even tell person say you dey come." It was one statement after the other in broken English.

He was sure he had never met his new companion who posed such unwelcome familiarity.

He observed quietly that the young man was only a lead and realized that more was to come. There were clusters of young men who also quietly observed what was going on which made Obodom realize he had to decide fast how to free himself from the impending danger. He was one of the urchins that were in the neighbourhood he found himself.

"My friend how you dey?" He felicitated with him, also in broken English with a pretended big understanding grin on his face.

"You suppose dey really know person when you see am. No be so them dey run things now! You suppose dey observe matter well before anything.

"You suppose be loyal, just come tell me big bros make you arrange things for me. You suppose know say, I go feel you immediately.

"Anyway, things never spoil. Every one dey make mistake some times. No wahala, take this five hundred Naira take hold body.

" You no even lift my load. You leave me dey carry my own bag. You fall hand well! Abeg, quick find me moto. I get some urgent runs.

"Make you look my face well as I no dey quick remember person. Next time when you see me just hail me make we two go relax somewhere" Obodom concluded shoving the man playfully on the shoulder.

His detractor was indeed disoriented not expecting such interactions. It was also not a bad deal for him none the less. Without taking much risk, he got five hundred naira. He immediately became apologetic

"My senior bros, no vex"- meaning my superior brother I am sorry

Happily, he carried his bag and escorted him to board a taxi.

It was actually a gambit of Obodom. He has only let the man understand he was aware of his threat much as he did not come out openly. He had mildly and playfully reprimanded that he would have shown some respect. That if he had been good on the job he was supposed to have realized he was not the type to be confronted. He cautioned him that it would have been better to come to him directly and request for some assistance without any threat. He further reprimanded that he did not even border to assist him to carry his luggage which is Nigerians' way of showing respect to their superior or senior.

He was happy that with only five hundred Naira and his wits he was able to secure his freedom.

He could not help wondering what would have been his ordeal if he had handled the situation differently. He evaluated his risk?

To him all that was no longer important. He recalled his late mother's situation as at the time she was robbed and violated.

Surprisingly the bitterness of the memory of his late mother was gone. In its place was now a burning desire to make a difference for the down trodden and the indigents of the society. They have lost their dreams as humans. Hope has eluded them. He must let them realize once more that *when there is a will there is a way.*

The good future they desired was only possible or impossible in line with belief.

When expectations good or evil was clothed in unwavering desire and passion, it must also unwaveringly come to pass. It was the greatest personal disservice allowing or exercising any fear of the unwanted and the unexpected.

Personal studies of the life of great men of this world have revealed a similar trend. This trend has never changed whether the endeavour was in politics, sciences or technology. The size, status or level of accomplishment also did not change the pattern.

Who wills will win. A traveller who permits no distraction will surely arrive at his destination irrespective of his speed. If you desire to arrive, you must first and foremost be set to go. He that fails to go should not expect to arrive. He must also not envy him that arrived because he travelled. The strength to persevere on a journey comes from the beauty, tranquil, serene and peaceful nature of the expected destination.

It can be called 'day dreaming, idle thinking, building of castle in the air' or similar demeaning names. However the dreams of the co-workers of God in times past that traversed this earth and are dead, are the harvests-of-comforts of modern times.

Look out for nations that lack dreamers and you have seen one devoid of development and progress.

We aspire to be as our heroes and heroines both living and dead but are we observant of the path of their lives journey. Can there be harvest without planting. Our Lord and Master have told us to seek and we will find and to knock for us to be granted access.

Nigeria is filled with great men and women who are heroes to great number of persons. Ask and you will hear unending names of heroes and heroines living and dead Aminu Kano; Balarabe Musa; Chukwuemeka Odumegwu Ojukwu; Chike Obi; Gani Fawehinmi; Adaka Boro; Ken Saro Wiwa; Humphrey Nwosu; Dora Akunyili; Ngozi Okonjo Iweala; Beko Rasome Kuti; Alex Ekwueme; GoodLuck Ebele Jonathan: Taribo West; Austin Jay Jay Okocha; Christian Chukwu; Mary Onyali; Ebenezar Obey; Dan Fulani; Peter Obi; Aliko Dangote; Chinua Achebe; Sam Loko Efe; Peter Rufai; Lamido Muhammadu Sanusi

A study of their beginning will present people, who the lazy; the non-ambitious will easily dismiss as those that can never become anybody in life. The understanding is not there that it is their passionate adherence to their dreams and not their humble or wealthy beginning that determined their future. Their humble or wealthy beginning was turned to be the light that led them to the future. It woke them up from slumber that 'to remain in the sinking ship meant they were going to drown'. They not only got off the ship but swam through the waves and tempest of the ocean of life until in safety they comfortably stood on the shore. They stood on the shore watching with pity those that refused their call to leave the sinking ship.

They were afraid of death and had refused to join them as they left the ship.

'We won't come with you. We will rather stay in the ship so that we will not drown' they answered.

They were not able to understand the tide of times. They interpreted their floating ship as an endless comfort not worth to be quit of. The effort of those that left the ship was interpreted to be a struggle that will end in death. It was too late when they realized that the ship was only the captors waiting prison of those that have been determined to die. Wise were the ones that left the ship, they belatedly realized. The death they were afraid that will befall them for leaving the ship was but a mirage the same way that the life they thought they clung to, staying back in the ship was also a mirage.

'What can I do to make a difference?

'What is it that can actually make a difference?' He was filled with worries. There were quite a lot on his mind. The more he tried answering the questions that came to his mind; the more there were to answer.

'Can I make the difference? Is there anything that I can do? He was deeply in thought. He imagined the great task it will be resolving the issues and challenges of the country even as he observed himself on the mirror. Who he saw was too fragile to solve anything.

Looking at himself and into his eyes in the mirror, he shouted out loud.

"I don't know how it will happen or perhaps what to do. I don't care how weak I seem. I don't want to know how it will happen – I must make a change. I swear, I must make a change. I must make a difference."

FIVE

• •

Kenneth Ofili Okolie was born with few advantages in life. His greatest advantage perhaps was having the kind of father he had. He appreciated him greatly. He was his hero. He had equipped him in life as no father ever does to his children. In raising his family too, he was determined to adhere to same system of upbringing hoping that his children will appreciate it as he did of his father.

It was only then that he was old that he could appreciate him. He had a different view of him when he was young. There were so many things he found difficult to understand. Against what was obtained with other children whose parents allowed playing as they willed, his was different. He was not allowed more than one and half hours play time daily. A day came that he was abruptly stopped from playing while other kids were still busy enjoying themselves. In subdued anger, he asked his father, 'Why don't you allow us to play like other fathers allow their children?'

'My son, time will come when you will understand. The pleasant things of life are the killers, run away from them if you ever want to be any body in life. Play is fun but will you play for the entire day? Are there no other things to do? What about your chores in the house. Is it your mother that will do everything? Are we not supposed to help each other so that the work will not be too much for some persons? It's just like sleep, sleep is fun, but you need not sleep the entire day or you will die of hunger. Progress comes not out of indulging oneself in the pleasurable things of life but out of productive effort. Such productive efforts don't come from merriment'

His father is never tired of explaining over and over again. He had wondered what stopped him from being a teacher. Any question on anything extorts thorough and detailed explanation from him except it is something he does not understand. Even in such instances he will promise to seek clarification. He would often call them as promised drawing their attention to their inquest even when they had forgotten to explain to them as promised.

It was therefore natural that he took encouragement from all that he learnt from him. When matters take a challenging turn, he often encouraged himself from his late father's teachings.

The full event concerning Kenneth Ofili Okolie can only be properly understood by going back to the events of the Asaba massacre. It occurred in the early October 1967 during the Nigerian civil war or to put it in a clearer context, Nigeria-Biafra war. What was then known and referred to as Federal troop who was unable to differentiate them from the intended brake away Biafran troop reportedly entered Asaba around October 5th, began entering searching houses and killing civilians, claiming they were Biafran sympathizers. Leaders summoned the town's people to assemble on the morning of October 7th hoping to end the violence through a show of support for 'One Nigeria.'

Hundreds of men, women, and children, adorned in white attire which they often wear in ceremonies of high esteem were gathered along the main street, singing, dancing and chanting 'One Nigeria.' At a junction, men and teenage boys were separated from women and young children and gathered in an open square at Ogbe-Osawa village. Federal troops then revealed machine guns, and orders were given to open fire.

Among the people that were gathered was Kenneth Ofili Okolie. His wife was also among the gathered. All they wanted was peace. By the time the Federal troops were made aware that they were not involved in the war the better and safer for them all. Victory can never be complete in war. Even as a victor there are always loses to count after the victory.

It is a long time indeed, but certainly not too long to erase the memory of the massacre of 700 men and boys by the Nigerian troops. While so many Nigerians may have forgotten about the Civil war and continued their lives, the victims of the war on both sides and especially the Asaba people, that genocide against their brethren has remained indelible in their minds. Many are still hurting terribly. The story had passed on from parents to their children of the bitter and painful memories of the incident.

The government had made no effort to appease the pains of the community and perhaps given the few surviving direct victims the opportunity to shed the tears of genuine reconciliation and forgiveness.

The stories are told in a hushed manner. It portends unspoken fear of a repeat should any one venture to mention it. Folk tales were replaced with despicable stories of human inhumanity to man. Tears often flowed when the stories are told. The quietude of 'who will tell our story if we do not? Even when we do, who will fight our case and who will grant us justice?' This tends to make quite a number of the victims succumb to the pressure to keep quiet and not talk about it.

Back in that faithful day Kenneth Ofili Okolie looked around and saw machine guns all around them.

'What is the meaning of all these? What is our offence? We are not in any war with anybody. We are only here to peacefully welcome them and let them know we are a peaceful community. Is this why we have to die?' He wondered in confusion.

One of the soldiers shouted the order to shoot and the sporadic sound of guns and the shrieking painful agony of the victims as they were hit by the bullets filled the air.

Sergeant **Adamu Kadiri** was among the Nigerian soldiers that have been ordered to shoot. As his eyes fell on Kenneth Ofili Okolie and his young wife, Deborah he was reluctant to carry out the commandant's orders. There was no doubt in his mind that as far as the military was concerned; the rule of the game was to obey the last order.

'Must the order be obeyed even if it contravenes the rule of military engagement?' He wondered. 'These people are no soldiers. They do not even belong to Biafran territory that Nigeria is fighting. By all principles of fairness: their community falls within the Nigerian territory and as such they are also Nigerians. Why then must they be killed for no reason other than they are of the same ethnic extraction as some of the Biafrans?'

It was obvious to him the discomfiture of the man as to how to protect his wife. It was not lost on him the obvious love that existed between the couple. 'And my command is to kill him?' He asked no one in particular.

There and then he made up his mind that he will never carry out the order. It was equally obvious to him that whether it was by his bullet or someone else, the man must surely die. The command has been given, not a boy or a man was to be spared.

He was in thought. What will he do to save the situation? If only he had been the general officer commanding the entire troop, he would not have given such an order. It was actually a war crime punishable by the Geneva Convention on military engagement.

He was still in thought when the blast of gun firings came in their sporadic and chaotic rhythms and He saw him fall.

He was not the only one that noticed he had been shot. Deborah, the wife also did and ran towards him. Adamu sprang into action immediately. He won't ever allow her to be hit too by bullet.

'Go away,' He yelled at her running towards her at the same time.

'Why have you killed my husband? What have we done to you people? What is our crime in arranging to host you people?' He heard her screaming from the distance.

It was one question after the other muttered in bitter quick succession as her tears flowed endlessly.

There was nothing to tell her. He understood her anger and bitterness. No one would have felt differently. The sound of the guns stopped abruptly. There was no command to stop. There was no single person standing anymore. Neither was there any movement among the casualties on the ground. All are supposed to be dead then. He looked to see what had become of the lady.

'Was she also hit by the bullet?' He wondered. She lay still besides the body of her husband. He wished he could go to find out what had become of her.

He suddenly realized that there had not been any shot from his gun and suddenly gave out three staccato blasts into the sky. A couple of the soldiers also did same as if to celebrate the carnage not understanding that his was shot out of utter frustration.

It was also getting to dusk and some of his fellow soldiers were whispering about some booties to harvest later when the order to recede has been issued.

In disgust he reflected on what they meant by booties. Plans and anticipations were actually on how to conscript the ladies as sex slaves. An entire community were in agony because of the brutal murder of their men folk and all there was to think about was sex with the same locals that their relations have just been murdered. He could not help wondering what got him into this mess.

It was not just being in a mess. The end of it all was what no one can foretell. When it had degenerated to the extent of murdering of innocent civilians outside the rules of Geneva Convention on military engagement he needed not being told that the end result was nothing palatable. There was no justification for the slaughtering of such number of persons for no reason other than that they speak same language with your perceived enemies.

While he had no power to determine the outcome of anything, he was determined to seek out the lady that the husband has been shot and see what help he could render. He was not there to assist his betrothed who perhaps would have been his wife; at the onset of the crises that he feared was murdered. He could not do anything because he was not there. In fact, he could not certainly say what happened to her. It was just that she could no longer be seen. Since the trend was that people of eastern extraction residing in the north were being killed by their northern hosts, it could rightly be assumed she had been killed.

Much as he was aware that he did not deliberately abandon her to be harmed, he still found it difficult to forgive himself. The memory had been such a disturbing one that he was not sure he would ever marry again. Juan was such a loving and pleasant person. She was so naturally suited by her profession because her second nature was to care and nurse. It was that quality in her that made his mother fall in love with her and naturally cultured him to equally fall in love with her.

She was however gone with the ethnic rivalry madness which had further degenerated into war. He won't ever set eyes on her anymore. She would have cursed whatever made her parents to come to Northern Nigeria.

He could not help wondering time and time again what went through her mind at those moments of her travail.

'Was she expecting me to come to her rescue? What would have been her feeling when she waited and waited but could not see me?'

Tears dripped down his cheek realizing the agonizing pain she must have gone through.

SIX

• •

It was January 15ᵗʰ 1966. He had just tuned in on his radio to listen to the news and was surprised at the broadcast he heard. A military coup against the constitutionally elected government was being broadcast on the radio.

'In the name of the Supreme Council of the Revolution of the Nigerian Armed Forces, I declare martial law over the northern Provinces of Nigeria. The constitution is suspended and the regional government and elected assemblies are hereby dissolved.

'All political, cultural, tribal and trade union activities, together with all demonstrations and unauthorised gatherings, excluding religious worship, are banned until further notice. The aim of the Revolutionary Council is to establish a strong united and prosperous nation, free from corruption and internal strife. Our method of achieving this is strictly military but we have no doubt that every Nigerian will give us maximum cooperation by assisting the regime and not disturbing the peace during the slight changes that are taking place. I am to assure all foreigners living and working in this part of Nigeria that their rights will continue to be respected. All treaty obligations previously entered into with any foreign nation will be respected and we hope that such nations will respect our country's territorial integrity and will avoid taking sides with enemies of the revolution and enemies of the people. My dear countrymen, you will hear, and probably see a lot being done by certain bodies charged by the Supreme Council with the duties of national integration, supreme justice, general security and property recovery. As an interim measure all permanent secretaries, corporation chairmen and senior heads of departments are allowed to make decisions until the new organs are functioning, so long as such decisions are not contrary to the aims and wishes of the Supreme Council. No Minister or Parliamentary Secretary possesses administrative or other forms of control over any Ministry, even if they are not considered too dangerous to be arrested. This is not a time for long speech-making and so let me acquaint you with ten proclamations in the Extraordinary Orders of the day which the Supreme Council has promulgated.

'These will be modified as the situation improves. You are hereby warned that looting, arson, homosexuality, rape, embezzlement, bribery or corruption, obstruction of the revolution, sabotage, subversion, false alarms and assistance of foreign invaders, are all offences punishable by death sentence. Demonstrations and unauthorised assembly, non-cooperation with revolutionary troops are punishable in grave manner up to death. Refusal or neglect to perform normal duties or any task that may of necessity be ordered by local military commanders in support of the change will be punishable by a sentence imposed by the local military commander. Spying, harmful or injurious publications, and broadcasts of troop movements or actions, will be punished by any suitable sentence deemed fit by the local military commander. Shouting of slogans, loitering and rowdy behaviour will be rectified by any sentence of incarceration, or any more severe punishment deemed fit by the local military commander. Doubtful loyalty will be penalised by imprisonment or any more severe sentence. Illegal possession or carrying of firearms, smuggling or trying to escape with documents, valuables, including money or other assets vital to the running of any establishment will be punished by death sentence. Wavering or sitting on the fence and failing to declare open loyalty with the revolution will be regarded as an act of hostility punishable by any sentence deemed suitable by the local military commander. Tearing down an order of the day or proclamation or other authorised notices will be penalised by death. This is the end of the Extraordinary Order of the Day which you will soon begin to see displayed in public. My dear countrymen, no citizen should have anything to fear, so long as that citizen is law abiding and if that citizen has religiously obeyed the native laws of the country and those set down in every heart and conscience since 1st October, 1960. Our enemies are the political profiteers, the swindlers, the men in high and low places that seek bribes and demand 10 percent; those that seek to keep the country divided permanently so that they can remain in office as ministers or VIPs at least, the tribalists, the nepotists, those that make the country look big for nothing before international circles, those that have corrupted our society and put the Nigerian political calendar back by their words and deeds.

Like good soldiers we are not promising anything miraculous or spectacular. But what we do promise every law abiding citizen is freedom from fear and all forms of oppression, freedom from general inefficiency and freedom to live and strive in every field of human endeavour, both nationally and internationally. We promise that you will no more be ashamed to say that you are a Nigerian. I leave you with a message of good wishes and ask for your support at all times, so that our land, watered by the Niger and Benue, between the sandy wastes and gulf of guinea, washed in salt by the mighty Atlantic, shall not detract Nigeria from gaining sway in any great aspect of international endeavour. My dear countrymen, this is the end of this speech. I wish you all good luck and I hope you will cooperate to the fullest in this job which we have set ourselves of establishing a prosperous nation and achieving solidarity.'

He was transfixed to his seat in confusion. It was indeed baffling as well as strange to him. The celebration of the independence of the country was just about 6 years old. He was not sure anything like that has happened anywhere, at the least to the best of his knowledge.

"Where will all these lead us to?" Adamu could not make anything out of the broadcast he had just listened to. One way or the other he feared there was going to be trouble.

"There is no need for all this," he thought further. He realized that the military are not meant to govern. They are only trained to protect the territorial integrity of nations against external aggression and invasion. There will be no body to perform their constitutional duties to the nation if they are allowed to start dabbling into national governance and administration.

Things followed up one another in very quick succession. It was no longer safe for people to inhabit places of their choice. Killings commenced around the nation and there was great fears palpitation and tribulation for individuals inhabiting locations other than their tribal and regional territories.

He was particularly concerned and for a good reason too, over the tragic incidences occurring all over the nation. He was still engaged in the battle with his potential family-in-laws who never wanted to entertain any idea of having their daughter married to another tribe.

"Are you telling me there are no ladies beautiful enough for you to marry among your tribe?" Her mother has asked him time and time again.

"My son," she tried to explain further. "I know you love my daughter. I am also aware that my daughter has so much love for you. In fact she would not have been able to mention it to anybody if not for the courage her love for you gave her. It is indeed difficult even for me. How on earth will I convince my husband to allow his daughter to marry a man of a different tribe?

32

"In our culture, it is not only the husband that marries his wife so to say apart from the conjugal intimacies. Can your love shield her from the vagaries of your relations who may not like her talk less of having her as a wife to their relation. That I am discussing with you in the first instance is because I am respectful of your mother's love for my daughter. However, I am still at lost as to how to handle or resolve this."

He had first met Juan at the municipal health centre. She was working as a nurse there while Adamu came with his sick mother. The chance existed for the medical care givers not to understand their language. Where that is the situation someone will be required to do the interpretation between the two. Where the interpreter does not have good understanding of English, it was often a daunting task for the patient to receive adequate treatment as relevant to him or her.

He had never met anyone that had her demeanour previously. She approached his mother with a comforting smile as she assisted her sit comfortably.

"Good morning," she greeted in their local dialect. "Please sit. Tell me how you are feeling?"

His mother was so happy hearing her. Obviously she was not from their region it therefore impressed her greatly that she took interest in a language not her own. Quite naturally they became friends. Her friendship to his mother was so endearing that she became the darling of the entire family with Adamu becoming the greatest beneficiary, they became lovers.

No one objected to their relationship. His mother had literally taken Juan as her daughter.

'My daughter born of another woman,' she joked with her most often and always coveted her company.

Juan herself was surprised as how she fell in love with Adamu. It was not that she really minded, realizing how much she loved him. That was her least of concerns. There were not many men that were as caring and loving as he was. He had not seen not even among his tribe's men.

"Do you think we understand what we are doing?" She once asked him.

"What exactly do you mean?" He asked her.

33

"You are Hausa and I am an Igbo. I cannot deny the fact that I am lucky your mother fell for me first or you would not have had the courage to love me realizing how difficult it usually is to get the consent of parents for such inter-tribal relationships. I can therefore say that the huddle had been scaled on your side.

"What about your extended family members? Will they tolerate me and then what about my own parents? They are definitely going to resist the relationship. Will you be tolerant of their rejection to weather the storm? Will you or will you abandon me eventually to my faith now that I have been enslaved to you by my love? I find it extremely difficult thinking of my future without you."

She was in tears. The horror of family rejection or abandonment by the man she has come to love so much was very troubling.

Adamu said nothing. He looked at her fully understanding what she was saying. Gently he pulled her closer allowing her to sob in his arms while his mind profusely wondered and trembled at the reality of her fears. There was no doubt in his mind that it would be worse for him if her fears turned out to be true.

"I understand all you have said. I may not know the extent of the rejection of your family. There is no way I can predict how much they will hate me for taking away their angel. The one thing I know however is that am determined to stand with you and for you no matter what happens.

"I may be worried they will reject me. I may be worried they will hate me. In all these, I will derive my strength that you will be with and for me as well. I am strengthened by the realization that I love you and you feel same for me."

She clasped her arms tighter around his waist. That was all she wanted and it was all that mattered. With him with her, she can never worry over any other thing.

SEVEN

• •

The glare of the early morning sun through the window woke Adamu up. He had slept long and well in the night but that didn't reflect on the way he felt. There was every reason for him to feel happy and relieved. He had a very eventful evening with Juan. He had gone straight to bed immediately after escorting her home. Their discussions were very hopeful as it was for their future together. His mind was extremely busy thinking about all that they discussed. Juan had felt that it was necessary to find a way to enable him get acquainted with her father. She was absolutely sure that her father will like him as a person. However, she was equally sure that it will be too much of a shock to confront him with the idea of her marrying someone that is not from her tribe.

Together they decided on their plan. He was still reviewing every little bit of the plan before he slept off.

With that as the last he had on his mind before he slept off he was expectant that he would have woken up cheerful, but that was not the case.

'So what could have happened to make him so downcast?' He worried as he made his way to work.

He was relieved when he arrived at work. As soon as he entered staff room, the hustle and bustle of the daily chores cleared his mind of all worries. The daily routine of an infantry soldier provides no luxury of idle emotional hiccups.

Their office routine was changed abruptly by an unexpected event to the chagrin of all. It was about 10am in the morning and there were an unprecedented number of people coming to the barracks. They were of two sets. The first set were the villains trying to run to safety while the second were the aggressors that were bent on inflicting as much harm on the other as could be possible.

It took time before the exact situation could be appreciated. Riot has broken out in the town. The city has split into two, the indigenes and the visitors. The indigenes were attacking the non-indigenes who have only anticipated their point of safety to be the military barracks and the police stations in the town.

Some were lucky to make it while others were not so lucky and were killed before even they could leave their houses. There were equally some that lost their lives from the stampede that the situation engendered.

The major concern of Adamu and his colleagues was to ward off the aggression against the non-indigenes within the barracks. It was becoming increasingly difficult doing so as the crowd kept increasing. He had more on his mind than his colleagues however.

'Where is Juan and what is happening to her?' The chaos in the city was the fall out of the military coup that had just taken place. It started to dawn on him that it was the premonition of the events of the day that kept him moody. He was obviously too worried to concentrate on anything anymore. It was difficult for him to be focussed on anything. If only there was a way he will know what is going on with her.

It was like ages for him to wait for close of work. He could not in any way afford to delay until then. He explained his concern to his commandant who willingly excused him. He dashed out in a hurry not knowing exactly what to do.

'Where am I going to look for her?' He wondered.

Finally he set to go to her work place, the city's medical centre. Just like the barracks the place was very rowdy. The difference there however was that the rowdiness was as a result of numerous patient waiting for medical attention. They were all of various degrees of physical injuries. Most of them were agonising in pain not knowing when there turn will come to be attended to.

She was supposed to be on duty but was not there. He would have seen her if she was there. She was so passionate about her job and about helping people. There was no way she would not have been seen trying to attend to the patients, if she was there. He would have been able to see her having waited that long.

'Perhaps, she did not eventually come to work,' he excused.

'But why won't she come to work?' He asked no one in particular as he made his way to their house. He turned back after a while. 'She could be within and in attendance to a patient' He reasoned. Luckily he saw Amina emerging from the ward.

"Please have you seen Juan?" He asked.

"She has not reported for work today. With what is actually going on I will not have advised her to even come." She responded to further aggravate his fears and worries. There was no choice left other than going to her house and he no longer hesitated in doing so. Every urgency is required now to trace her where about and condition.

There were no commuters to take him to her house. 'Was it the lack of transport that prevented her from going to work?' He wished that would be the reason as he trekked on the road that unusually had become very lonely and deserted.

The road was littered at some spots with human corpses. In some locations with scattered and damaged wares from shops within the vicinity. Some houses were burnt down while some others are still burning from the attack of arsonists.

He never wanted to give up on her or her family. His hopes were however failing him based on the things he had seen so far. What he saw on the road gave him no succour but he persisted. He will not bear the imagination that she was somewhere waiting for his assistance and he never showed up.

'She would do everything possible to wait for me.' He encouraged himself and kept going.

He suddenly stopped. Smouldering in front of him was their house. There were some household items from the house littered around.

'Who could have done this? Where is everybody?' There were so many questions begging for answers. He hardly knew which answer he needed proffered before the other.

He was too scared to believe his fears. By now he was very scared. The area that used to be extremely busy had become so deserted and empty that he had not encountered one person all the time he was there. There was no one or anybody to enquire from. 'If all this could just happen like that, it must have been pre planned. How was it that no one heard about it?' If such plans had been made, how could the police intelligence not pick it up? The carnage would not have happened if the police were privy of it except there was connivance with the perpetrators. 'Could that have been the case?' He wondered.

'No, no", he reasoned. An institution of the state whose duty it was to protect lives and property of the citizenry cannot connive with hoodlums to perpetrate such level of havoc.

The only thing of any significance he found was Juan's photograph lying on the ground. It was her photograph in her nursing uniform. He put it inside his pocket as he headed home fully aware that all was not well anymore. 'Where have they gone to or perhaps what happened to them?'

He was all in thought. The turn of events in the country was gruesome as they were unfortunate. A counter coup had occurred after the first. The first had been taken to have favoured a particular set of people and put them to an advantage. The second was carried out to balance out the ills of the first as perceived by the perpetrators.

Be it the first or the second the victims are always the same. The perpetrators are often prepared for the outcome of their actions. The generality of the masses are neither aware of their intended actions nor were they prepared for the outcome. They are the ones that surfer the consequences. They are often ill equipped to safeguard themselves.

A lot of people lost their lives. The ones that are alive have lost their shelter and means of livelihood. All they had wanted was just to live their simple lives.

'What has Juan got to do with all these? What have her family members got to do with it. What offence have they committed and who have they offended to deserve the tragedy that had befallen them. What actually happened to them?'

He went straight to his mother when he got home. It was obvious to him from her countenance that she was aware of the happenings in town. Her look at him was so intent. He knew what she intended to ask but could not.

'That means Juan had not come to hide in their house to escape the danger in the town.' He concluded in desperation.

"I don' know where Juan is. I have not been able to see nor locate her. I have gone to her work place, she was not there. I have gone to her house; the house has been burnt down."

There was no need to continue. His mother had collapsed and would have fallen on her face if he had not run to her rescue. He was suddenly facing more than he could handle. He sought assistance from his siblings to lay her down comfortably.

He was not aware his mother had such love for Juan and this made him feel greater sense of lost than he had ever felt in the past. If only he knew what happened to her. With that yet to be resolved his mother had collapsed at the news of the disappearance of Juan and what befell her family.

In any case, his mother eventually regained consciousness but refused to talk to anyone. She preferred to be left alone. Somehow it was as if she held Adamu responsible for what had befallen Juan. He quite agreed with her.

'If I have been there with her I would not have let anyone touch her nor set their house of fire.' He regretted. 'I was not there when she needed me most and how on earth will I know what have become of her?'

'Why won't the citizens of this country live by the tenets of the words of her national anthem?' He further wondered as he thought through the words of the national anthem;

He was particularly sobered by the statement that *'though tribe and tongue may differ, in brotherhood we stand.'* The tribes and tongue are indeed quite diverse and different but the underlying truth still remained that they are all humans. Blood flows in their systems and all are still prone to same human weaknesses as every other person. Just as Juan would have felt if anything happened to him was exactly the pain he was going through.

He further thought about the last stanza of the anthem which was like a prayer soliciting **'God to grant this our one request. Help us to build a nation where no man is oppressed.'** How could a nation with such national anthem still live and allow the oppression of one another.

His mother had been withdrawn and dejected for the fact that no one knew the fate of Juan. Because they have allowed love between themselves it has become real to them that she is a human. They were mourning the grave ill that had befallen her and the rest of her family members. She is not from the Northern part of Nigeria. Some people of the Northern extraction within Nigeria inflicted such grave hurt of the extent that were yet to be fully comprehended on her and her family. Probably there may not be anyone of her relations aware of what befell them. If that was the case, there was no one of the Eastern extraction of Nigeria mourning them. Some people however, not related to her biologically but bonded to her emotionally are in terrible pains on account of her misfortune. These people are of the same Northern extraction, same as the people that caused the harm in the first instance.

The senselessness of the entire situation made him angry and terribly agitated.

'Why then will my own brethren supposedly taking a revenge on my behalf had hurt me so terribly?' He wondered bitterly.

'Do they appreciate the level of bitterness they are afflicting others with? Who, if any had benefited from these grave atrocities committed?'

There was no way he could make out any sense out of the situation. He was also aware that the problem had just started. Right from the moment the first coup of 15th January 1966 was announced and the counter coup of 29th July 1966 that followed, there had been that unease in him. He was apprehensive that nothing good will ever follow.

From all he was witnessing there was no strong indication that anything will ever be settled or resolved. Bitterness was so deep and anger so enshrined in the heart of the various ethnic nationalities of the country. There were so much loses to be countered by all. Suddenly it appeared there was no reason to have brought the various people and cultures into a single entity called Nigeria. All the joy, merriment and happiness of 1st October 1960 when Nigeria got its independence had suddenly evaporated.

The same people who were in unison in their request that Britain should go and leave them to govern themselves are then fighting themselves. It suddenly appeared as if actually that maturity has not been attained for the independence of the country in the first place.

'Britain had intentionally left some cleavages of divide to make the nation not to last,' some had often argued. 'It was the revenge they took on Nigeria and Nigerians for ever requesting for independence,' they further buttressed their argument.

'Since that is the case and we are aware, why should we be as stupid still as to fall a victim?' others were quick to counter such argument. Whoever is wrong or right does not really matter or count anymore, Adamu is the confirmed looser.

One thing led to another and on May 30th 1967 the Eastern Region of Nigeria seceded and became Republic of Biafra. More things happened and on July 6th 1967 a full blown war started. The Nigerian civil war started with Adamu Kadiri fighting a war he would ordinarily not be involved in. It made no sense to him in anyway what was being fought for.

He was questioning the right of the state to foist war on its citizens. He was deprived of his love, Juan and then drafted to fight a war that will bring about more death and pains on people. He could not help but regret the day he joined the military. It was not in him to fight an unjust war. Unfortunately it was not for him to decide the wars he fights as a soldier. All that he was trained to do was to obey the last command. The last command unfortunately then was to shoot innocent civilians. Once more he is witnessing the agony of lovers being separated by violence for no fault of theirs. They wronged no man and committed no crime but yet they were punished by death.

As his mates planned their escapade, he had just one plan and nothing else. He would definitely go and trace the lady. He was aware there was nothing he could do to bring back her husband to life. However, he was just curious to satisfy himself that she did not also fall by their bullet. He was sure he saw her fall. Whether the fall was in share agony of frustration at what had befallen her or that she was hit by the bullet, he could really not tell. He was determined to find out.

He waited for his colleagues to leave. He was on a sole visit not intending to have any company. There was no way he can explain to any one of them what he was going for or what he intended to do. If he explained to them, no one will understand. It will make no sense to them. It was equally of no importance to them. They will equally not understand why he was so concerned about a stranger for that matter.

He also could not help wondering if he was doing the right thing. Was there really anyway he could be of any assistance to her even then that he realized the spouse was dead.

"Does it really matter whether I can do anything for her or not?" He asked no one in particular. "Let me just get to the place," he encouraged himself as he picked his direction with some of the landmarks he remarked.

He noted that the community was still in mourning as he went. There were still some agonizing yelp from time to time and from different locations as if it was then they realized the tragedy that befell them. Each time he reviewed the occurrences his mind inadvertently wondered about Juan. There was no longer any doubt in his mind that she and the family members were no more.

There he was effecting the decisions of the state in the war. Lives were being wasted unjustly and for unjust course for that matter. He was now in the midst of Juan's tribes men. It would have been consoling if the visit was in condolence for the death of their brethren. Instead they were inflicting greater harm on them.

He was engrossed in his thought and was brought to alertness by the sound of some murmuring and crying. The community had come to the scene of the massacre to gather and evacuate the corpses of their kinsmen who had been killed in cold blood. It was obvious they were still scared of further onslaught and occasionally screened their surrounding for unwanted visitation.

Adamu wavered into an adjoining bush to escape detection. There was no gain saying the level of danger he was exposed to. He knew they will gladly take their revenge on him if discovered and made sure he was completely out of view. He was very certain of the location of his interest and gently searched out a closer location from where he could have a better view.

There he found who he was looking for. He was happy to realize she was not dead like the husband. However, she will still not let go of his corpse. All effort to console her was proving abortive.

"Oh! My dear God, why let him die? He has wronged no one and defrauded no one. What is his offence? Why would you permit him to die?" She kept wailing as they made effort to separate her from the corpse.

He put his face to the earth in sadness. He could feel the pangs of her bitterness. Her pains were so real to him because of his experience. He never wanted to see anymore. His heart was broken not just for her but also in remembrance of Juan. There was simply so much bitterness in life that he wondered if there were really any good reason to be alive.

What was the worth of life while humans are inflicting so much pain on each other? Where would all these lead to but agony and sufferings. Then that he became aware that she was still alive, he wondered the quality of her life thenceforth. From all that happened and all that he witnessed, he realized how difficult it was going to be for her to live without him.

'May be time will heal her pains,' he resolved. It was now time to find his way back to join the others. He could not afford to stay longer than he had. He would not want to be left by the division. He was left with mixed feelings. On one hand he felt fulfilled that he was able to find out what had become of her and at least happy that she was not also fell by the bullet. On the other hand he was also angry and unhappy that the happiness of her life had been distorted. She was so neurotic in her anguish and wondered if she was still sane. No one can foretell whatever would become of her. What he knew however as at that point in time was that she was in terrible bitterness and agony at the murder of her spouse.

EIGHT

• •

Barrister Ahmed Nasser had made some progress with Osayiwmense's mother. Apart from progress made in officially enabling Obodom to be the guardian of Osayiwmense, he had also facilitated her undergoing thorough medical examination to determine the nature of treatment she will be given.

"She is suffering from a combination of different factors," explained the Doctor. "Primarily, it was discovered that she has the syndrome of Dissociative Amnesia resulting not from direct damage to the brain but from psychological causes. She may have gone through a traumatic experience in addition. This represses the memory making it difficult to recall information, usually from the moment of the traumatic and stressful occurrence in the person's life.

"Still being investigated is the madness factor. She is not violent and responds naturally to emotional overtures as any other person. She is expected to undergo some more complex and rigorous tests by which better conclusions will be made and appropriate treatment decided."

"Do I take this to mean that we should be hopeful of total recovery?" Obodom asked.

"While carrying out diagnosis aimed at resolving the psychopathic disorder, I will immediately commence treatment on the amnesia that is the memory loss.

"I will say that there are quite some chances of her full recovery. Let me complete all necessary checks first."

"Of course, talking about the treatment, amnesia has no specific or known treatment of its own. What is done however is to attempt to treat the underlying cause of the ailment. In essence it is hoped that if the actual cause of the amnesia is treated, the patient is automatically healed. There is also this tendency that the patience when he or she relieves the earlier experience that caused the amnesia in the first instance, may suddenly recover from the memory loss completely.

"What is done therefore is to stimulate various presumable scenarios that can traumatize a person into amnesia to patients and monitor their reaction. When the right experience is re-enacted, the patient often becomes quite thoughtful.

This being the case, the particular scene is repeated in a measured frequency and doses until the patient is struck with sudden remembrance of all that were eluding their memory.

"Although improvements occur when patients receive certain treatments, there is still no actual cure or remedy for amnesia so far. To what extent the patient recovers and how long the amnesia will continue depends on the type and severity of individual cases. "

Obodom and Nasser were quite satisfied with the doctor's explanation and were expectant of full recovery for Osayiwmense's mother. Obodom was also concerned of what to expect after the recovery and hoped it was going to be for the good of the young boy. He wanted her to naturally fill the vacuum of a mother for the boy realizing that his future development depended greatly on that.

However, he had more than that on his mind. There were so many more like Osayiwmense and his mother within the society. A lot more than what he is doing as an individual is required. A lot more people have to be committed to the endeavour to change the narrative of the nation called Nigeria. Why has the nation not progressed as it ought to? Why should there be the likes of the boy and the mother in a nation blessed with so much resources? Is there really nothing that can be done? Are there no good people in the nation that should see things even from a better perspective than him?

The questions kept spinning out without answers. There was no doubt in his mind that he cannot do it alone. By whatever way and means possible, he must galvanize support from as many as can be favourably disposed to change Nigeria for the better. He was also aware that so many people have lost faith in the country. They may, based on their disappointing experiences not see or believe in the possibility that the narrative can ever change.

'There must be a way.' He encouraged himself. 'I must find that way no matter how long it would take. I must find a way to raise the hope of some that something can be done. I must show them the possibility of changing the story. Nations abound that are not as gifted as Nigeria and they are doing great. Just as it takes an individual believing in oneself to succeed, it also takes same for a nation to change the narrative for the better.'

As he moved to exit the hospital a poster pasted besides the gate post struck his attention. The poster was that of the students' union advertising the students' union week activities. He read through the advertorial and noted that there was a coming election in the university. The hospital where Osayiwmense's mother was undergoing treatment was actually a teaching hospital of the university.

There and then he concluded that it was the opportunity he was looking for. He will seek an opportunity to talk to the generality of the students. It would actually be of greater benefit to change the orientation and mind set of the youths. If their youthfulness, energy and zeal are harnessed into effort to restore the nation, there would be a radical change in the country.

'That is exactly what I will do,' he resolved.

He immediately intensified effort to get involved in the student week activities of the institution. His first move was to meet the students' union president. Luckily it was not difficult for him to get audience and arrangements were concluded for him to be the guest speaker on the manifesto day kick-off event. It was equally an opportunity for him to earnestly discuss with the student union president. He was not prepared for what was to come. The president of the union was a lady. He had to endeavour not to show his surprise in order not to create the impression he was a male chauvinist.

"I want you first and foremost to understand why I desire to talk to you and your fellow students. I am sure that as the student union president of this great university, you must have been confronted with the task of meeting the expectations of your colleagues. I know also that you must have equally been confronted with the need of your colleagues in their pursuit of their education. Excuse me however if I am not that coordinated, I earnestly has not expected a lady as the union president.

"Essentially too, you must have been elected by your colleagues because they believe you have better things to offer them as students in making things better for them when compared with others that contested with you. For you being a lady to survive the prejudice that would have created in the mind of your colleagues to win the position is no mare fit. Have I spoken correctly?"

"You are indeed correct. It was not my intention to vie for the students' union president. It was a chance occurrence that I got involved into students' unionism.

"A course mate was expelled with a few others for spearheading students' protest against the reduction by 2 hours of the guaranteed electric power supply time from 1 am to 11pm. Students were cajoled and threatened that more people will be expelled if they towed their footsteps.

"I was really disturbed when this happened as he was a personal friend. I could not understand why such an intelligent student will be expelled just because of championing such a noble course. I also know that he was barely getting by financially as a student with extreme self-denial by his parents. The parents go through great drudgery to make ends meet. I really loved him for his type of person. I was also aware how he humbly and diligently assisted his parents during holidays. The expectations of his parents were high on him and I needed no one to tell me the devastation it would have amounted to in his family.

"I must confess that I was more driven by these realities than any other thing I galvanized others to resist the expulsion. I personally requested audience with the Vice Chancellor after 3 days of peaceful nonattendance of lecture protest. Thanks to the solidarity of the entire students' body, the school authority rescinded the expulsion of the students. After the episode, quite a lot of the students insisted that I contest for the union's president. Coincidentally all these were happening at the period of students' union election time. It was indeed mostly the men who were insisting that I contest or else I would not have had the courage to do so. They kept assuring me that they will campaign for me and give me all the support I required to succeed. The actual turning point was when I eventually accepted, the two students who had earlier indicated their interest withdrew from the race."

"I am happy to hear this. I need you and so many others like you to rescue our country. It would definitely not come easy and it is also not an immediate thing. As I stand with you, I cannot tell you that in a year, two years or ten years it will be achieved. In fact, I will be more correct to say that it is a continuous task. That is why I need more people to come on board. That is why I want to talk to all of you. That is also why I want you to understand my mission and also make it your mission.

47

"I am indeed grateful that I have this opportunity. You however have one more thing to do for me immediately and many other things later. I want you to mobilize all the students if it is possible. Please do everything you can for the sake of our dear country."

'The dice is cast;' he thought 'there is no going back.' All that must be done has to be. The older generation has not done much to better the situation of the ordinary man. There was only selfishness in their orientation and disposition and nothing regarding the future of the nation is ever taken seriously. The great potentials of the nation are being allowed to waste while the lot of the weaker populace in the polity kept deteriorating on a daily bases. Time has come to rescue the situation and the youth has to be made aware of the excruciating and distasteful future that awaited them if they do nothing.

Obodom was very convinced that if he mobilized and galvanized the passion and strength of the youth in the project the older generation will be forced to realize how they have failed the nation and the conscientious ones among them would change and also join the vanguard of the redeemers of the project called Nigeria. He was excited at the erudite nature of the student union president, Mubo Awoyemi. Her manner of ascendancy to leadership was equally a complementary endorsement to the entire concept. That was the calibre and nature of leadership the nation was yearning for.

He marvelled at the turn out of events. By circumspect all things kept moving him to a future. One thing has often led to another and he cannot but ponder at the artistry of providence that honour the righteous desires and passions of men and women in the history of mankind to guide them to the fulfilment of their honourable desires. Things were evolving as a vehicle on auto cruise making him wonder who actually was directing the affairs of men.

He had not forgotten that he had only come to the University Teaching Hospital for the diagnosis of Osayiwmense's mother's medical situation. That had led to the realization that there was going to be a students' union elections and there he was already planning with Mubo Awoyemi on how to mobilize the students not just for election but to create an avenue to in plant new consciousness in the youths as to the need to redeem and take over their country for a better tomorrow for the upcoming generations.

Eventually the expected manifesto day came. The stage was set and all other arrangements concluded. Even Mubo was impressed at the turn out of students. From her rough estimation more than the sixteen thousand student population have gathered. The sports centre which was picked for the event was filled to the brim by students. It was not only the students that were gathered, the media both print and electronic and from within and outside the university were equally on ground to cover the event.

"You are indeed a great mobilizer," Obodom complemented her on arrival to the venue. He was actually taken aback to witness such a great crowd. He had to wonder at his own preparedness to address them satisfactorily.

'There is no time for further preparation,' he opined to himself.

When the time came it was Mubo that first ascended the podium.

She was beautiful, radiant and eloquent on stage. Obodom wished she would be the one to even deliver his own prepared speech wondering if he could do better than her.

"The greatest student of the greatest university," her voice bellowed on the microphone in greeting to the audience.

"Great," they chorused.

"Great, great, great," she started again.

"Great, great, great," they chorused and all started clapping in applause of their leader.

She raised a clenched fist in the air as a symbol of their greatness and the applause increased to a crescendo.

She suddenly opened her once clenched fist and gently swung her hand down and everywhere was quiet that one could hear the drop of a pin.

She graciously looked around in appreciation of their solidarity.

"Oh my God!' she exclaimed, "I love you. Believe me I greatly love you all.

"I will always appreciate you for your support and encouragement. You indeed imposed me on yourselves to guide your affairs. I happen to be the first female student union president that this nation has ever produced. I was terribly scared to venture into politics talk less of being the president of the students' union. You all insisted that I should go. I did not hide my fears from you. In fact, I screamed out my fears to you. I was even rude in my refusal to some of you but you all persisted and assured that you were going to go the whole length with me.

"I want to say thank you because you have kept that promise all the way. I wish myself that I could do better. You were still very kind in your judgement of me. You tolerated my weakness and encouraged my strength. Please do accept my unwavering gratitude to you all. For the two tenures that I led the student union, I was elected unopposed, what a love and what a support.

"Everything that has a beginning must also come to an end. This is why we are all mortals, for we have life and death. My tenure is coming to an end but the existence of this great university has not and will never come to an end. It must continue. Its greatness must also continue. For its greatness to continue, the greatness of the students themselves must continue. To ensure this we have all gathered here. We are here to kick-off the manifesto day. This is because we want to elect new executives and parliamentarians to our union. We are going to do the right thing and we are going to do it peacefully.

"As part of this our activity, we have in our mist a man of honour and integrity who will be speaking to us on the topic – ***Youths and The Journey to Nation Building***. Please in respect to his request, I will allow him to introduce himself. Please, a round of applause as I welcome to the podium, Obodom Agozie."

Everywhere was agog in applause especially for the love the students have for her and her radiant beauty and oratory. They were ready to welcome any one she welcomed. The students have indeed wanted her to nominate a candidate that will succeed her but she declined. They really loved her and kept applauding long after she had left the stage for Obodom.

"Before I introduce myself, I will want you once again to give a rousing ovation to your president. She is indeed a great leader. This country is greatly in need of leaders that will lead like her. We desire Leaders that are leaders indeed that the populace will gladly follow. It is this journey to find such leaders that had brought me to you.

"I am sure that you want leaders of this nation to lead like her. Once more please give her another round of applause.

"First of all I want to thank your president, your student union executives, your parliamentarians and indeed you the entire students for this opportunity to discuss with you on Youths and the journey to nation Building. I want you to also excuse me for requesting to introduce myself. It is not really that I have anything fascinating to introduce about myself. I want you rather to appreciate why we all have to jointly make that commitment to take back our country and redeem it and model it into one that will be for the good of all.

"I am alive because of the good of one woman. If all of us become good in our country it will go a long way in giving us that country of our choice that we will all cherish.

"I am Obodom Agozie. I have a mother whose name is Geraldine James. I know that you will wonder as I did as a boy growing up, why my surname is different from that of my mother? My surname is different from that of my mother because she was not my biological mother. The name of my biological mother was Juliana Agozie. She died after giving birth to me. My biological mother had all her heart for me in love and trust but had not the opportunity to show me the love. Geraldine was my mother that nurtured me to adulthood and thank God for her perhaps I would not have been alive. God realizing that my mother could not live planted me into the heart of my foster mother. She chose in honour of my late mother to keep her surname and to give me the name she made out from my biological mother's profession of her love for me. She proclaimed me to be 'Obodom' which meant her community, her nation or better still her world.

"At this stage every sane person will also be asking, 'who is your father?'

"My beloved, the truth is that I do not know him but I have an idea who he could possibly be. My father is a robber and a rapist. Two men raped my mother when she was barely 13 years old. They did not just rape her; they also robbed her of the money she got on the fateful day hawking her merchandise. First and foremost; she was sent out by a woman who was supposed to be her guardian to go hawking on the streets. After she was robbed and raped her guardian was more infuriated by her loss of money than the young girl's excruciating experience, she sent her out of her home. She did nothing to heal her emotional and physical violation. From then and throughout her period of pregnancy, for she became pregnant from being raped, she had no home but to wander the streets until her being delivered of me and eventually her death.

51

"I always choose to introduce myself by telling my story to honour these two wonderful ladies in my life. This is my story and I know there are many more in our society that have had a more mindboggling story than mine to tell. Even among you, there are still those whose stories are more inconceivable than mine. I should be ashamed telling such story, I however decided not to border.

"It is important that such stories be told to enable us ask ourselves some relevant and pertinent questions. We need to boldly confront the anomalies in our society or else we would not have any future for the coming generation.

"Are these things supposed to occur in a well ordered society? Should children who cannot protect themselves, who had better been in school be hawking merchandise in the streets of our country? Does it not matter to anybody that qualitative and affordable education should be the right of every child in this country? What kind of a nation are we going to have in the future if the level of poverty is growing on a daily bases unabated? What kind of a future are we going to have if as a nation we are not investing in the future of our children and the youths?

"Why am I talking to you? What is the need of all these? Youths and the Journey to Nation Building is apt as the theme of this discourse for several reasons. The youths have to appreciate the fact that they are key stakeholders in the project called Nigeria. Time has passed when they relax and expect someone else to put it right; no you have to do things by yourselves and for yourselves. I do agree that our leaders who coincidentally are our parents have every moral compulsion to put things right for you their children. Unfortunately, they are not broad minded enough to see the generality of the children and youth of the country as theirs. To them their children are just their biological children. They fail to see their responsibility to the rest citizens in their manner and nature of governance. This is why you have to get involved.

"It is also important that we start that journey now. Today is your manifesto day. It is expected that the various candidates who are contesting will be telling you their plans to make things better. First and foremost, I will want the contestants to realize that the journey to nation building has already commenced. They have to realize that it is a serious affair. The promises they are making are promises that must be kept. Those promises are not made because they want to win the election, they should be made because they are doable and they are committed to doing them.

"The rest of the students must also realize how serious this election is. They are to evaluate the candidates based on track record of what they have been able to do previously. They have to look at them from who they have been in the past. From that standpoint, they can now evaluate them to see whether they are in a position to do what they are promising to do. They are also to hold them accountable on those promises and checkmate them to ensure they keep their words. This is not only relevant here; it is also relevant in our larger society. We are to hold our leaders accountable. They hold whatever office they occupy to protect the interest of the populace. They are there to get things done. We must therefore begin to get involved in the affairs of this country. These are our affairs to deal with.

"If we challenge our political representatives to be up and doing; if we challenge them to be committed to the wellbeing of this country, things will change for the better. We must get involved and the time to get involved is now.

"Why do we have to get involved? We are getting involved because we cannot be playing the Ostrich who hides the head in the sand and assumes that it is save when the entire body is exposed and prone to danger. If the political leadership we have were responsive regards to their duties and obligations, we would not have the current situation where lots of youths that are supposed to be in the University are not either because their parents and guardians are jobless or are stricken with poverty and could not afford to send them to school.

"For this reason we have to do everything within our power and our means to ensure that whoever assumes any position of political leadership or any leadership position for that matter is both responsive and accountable to the people. If we don't do that we will have as a reward a worse society by the time we have graduated from school. This will also leave us not being able to afford the education of our own children.

"The most vicarious situation currently is that the youths are mostly playing the Ostrich game of 'it does not concern me and therefore it does not matter.' Sometimes the youths assume a more damnable position of ensuring that those who can do the job are not allowed the level playing ground of free, fair and credible election. This they do by offering themselves to the visionless politicians who have nothing to offer the citizens other than to loot our treasury as tugs to rig elections on their behalf. As we are all gathered here today, we must all say 'no' to that going forward. We must contribute our quota by ensuring that elections are free from violence, fair and credible. We must ensure that we are also involved by registering if we have reached the legal age to vote. We can also get involved by joining the political parties and contesting elections for the purposes of rendering services to the larger society. This should be the actual reason for vying for any position of leadership.

"We have to get involved and we have to get involved today and not tomorrow. We must take that solemn oat to move our country forward. There is no longer that time to waste. There is no one to create that future for us if we do nothing. There is no one or any other country that would build a nation for us if we don't. We can all now take that solemn decision to do something for our country and ourselves not to remain idle and indolent. We can create the world we want to live in. I Obodom Agozie do solemnly declare today that I am committed to a great Nigeria. I assure you of my commitment to this course. I swear my commitment to this course and want those that would come along with me to do likewise.

"I want today those great men and women who will commit themselves to this decision. I want today those men and women of courage who will declare with me that enough is enough. I want today those who will declare with me that we are not just going to fight this battle but must win. I want here today those who will stand out with me to say no to corruption in all ramifications. I want those that will stand out with me to put a stop to child labour and domestic violence. I want those that will stand out with me to say no to youth involvement in crimes.

"If you have made this solemn declaration with me and you are committed to it. If you have taken this oath of commitment on this course, I want you to show that support by singing our national anthem with me."

There was a thunderous and boisterous recital of the Nigerian national anthem as never before as all chorused in unison

NINE

● ●

The manifesto speech of Obodom Agozie sparked off political consciousness among the youths in Nigeria and pertinent questions and presentations became the rife of the day. With it also raised the questions of youth involvement in politics. Questions were also being asked about the relevance of some old politicians who were often recycled at every turn of political event of the country.

Newspaper headlines and commentary were rife with one thing or the other on the speech to mark the manifesto day of the university. One newspaper had a headline 'I SWEAR.' It then went further to chronicle the indolence of the nation's political leadership that had failed to understand the oath of service they swear to each time they take oath of office. It challenged them to learn from the youths who had shown their understanding and correctly too of what leadership is all about – service to the people. A vivid story of what transpired in the university's manifesto day address was narrated.

It went further to enumerate all the campaign promises made by the incumbent government with percentage evaluation of what had been accomplished of each promise after three years. It stressed its disgust that the greatest accomplishment of any of the promises made was 25% and wondered the justification for such government remaining in office. The opulence lifestyle of these politicians urgently questions whose purpose such leadership serves – the masses or the politicians.

This upsurge in clamour for accountable leadership however did not go down well with some who felt their political chances and opportunities were being eroded on a daily bases. The status quo must be maintained or they would go into political extinction. A way must be found for them to remain relevant and continue the exploitation of the polity. It was just a year to the end of their political tenure in office and they must act promptly enough to salvage the situation. A think-tank committee was set up on how to tackle and address the situation appropriately and immediately. It was mandated to submit its proposal within 3 days.

There was a surge in awareness of the populace. No day passed without the news of the displeasure of the people with the status quo. There was also increase in the demand of the organised labour in one sector or the other of the economy. The restiveness of the citizens was continuously on the increase. The government was suddenly on the edge seeking immediate amelioration of things to avert an imminent electoral defeat in the coming pols in a year's time.

Obodom was not unaware of the impact of his address to the university students. He was happy at the turn of events and was wondering at the next thing to do. He was kept on his toes because of the issues he have on his hands to resolve. These issues were constantly reminding him of the ills of the society which must be tackled if things are ever to change. Even as he waited patiently for the results of the medical diagnosis on Osayiwmense's mother, he was equally wondering at the next line of action that will have another improved and positive impact on the society.

He was in one such mood when looking out of his window he saw 2 vehicles stop in front of his house. He noted that the occupants of the vehicles were security personnel and wondered at what brought them. Apart from the driver, each of the vehicles had 2 other passengers, one in the front besides the driver and the other behind. He watched, still trying to understand the situation as the passenger in the front seat of the first vehicle alighted and made for his door while the rest remained seated as they were.

There was a knock on his door. He waited for a repeat before he responded.

"I will be with you in a moment," he responded taking the last look at them through his window as he moved to open the door.

"Who is it?" he asked as if he was unaware of who his visitors were.

"I am Sergeant Irabor from the State Security Service of the Presidential Villa"

"Good morning," greeted the Sergeant as he opened the door, "you are required at our office for some security discussions."

"Good morning," he responded. "This is really surprising to me. Me of all people required for some security discussions. When have I become this important?" He asked jokingly.

"You may not know how important you have become," reiterated the officer with a cynical smile.

"Give me a little time to dress up."

"That is Ok," replied the officer, closing the door gently by himself.

Immediately, he took a pen and a paper and scribbled:

2 vehicles with 6 security officers came to invite me 10:17hrs to their secretariat for security discussions. Don't really understand what for. The only clew I have of their identification is Sergeant Irabor, the particular officer that came to the door.

He put the message in an envelope addressed to Barrister Nasser and kept it on the floor so that it can be seen immediately on opening the door and stepped out, locked his door and followed them.

Sergeant Irabor showed him to the front seat of the first vehicle, closed the door after he had sat down and entered the seat behind him. They all drove out immediately after with crispy mare utterance from him of:

"They are mine colleagues."

There was complete silence from everyone as they drove to their secretariat. Obodom was apprehensive but remained quiet.

'If they wanted me dead they had enough time to do that,' he further encouraged himself fully aware that he would be made aware of the reason for the invitation on arrival to their destination.

He observed that the vehicle drove to the area known as GRA, Government Reserved Area. The area is usually where all the allied administrative organs of government are situated. There is also a security agency located there close to the seat of government to enable prompt security intervention where and when necessary. Nothing on all these was lost on him but he could not yet figure out the reason behind his invitation.

Irabor showed him to a well-furnished and air-conditioned office and conveniently and appropriately disappeared as he waited alone. He was asked to sit on a chair before a table. Behind the table was another chair obviously meant for the owner of the office, he imagined. There were 3 other chairs in the office. He was still assessing the office when the door opened and 2 men entered.

From their mannerism and look, he was certain that one was an officer and the other a civilian. He was still curious as for the reason of his invitation. There was nothing he was aware he did against the laws of nation. He was also not in any political party to worry about being tagged a political opponent which will earn him the toga of political victimization. In any case he was aware that His lawyer and friend must have seen his mail then.

Both have gotten well together. They have grown to become friends due to sharing the same outlook on a lot of things. Their values were virtually same so naturally other than just being personal solicitor to Obodom, they became very close friends. On an account that he visited at an occasion to hand over some documents for endorsement and he was not around, he decided to let him have a spare key to his apartment.

'If any harm befalls me, he can at least be aware.' He comforted himself when he remembered that they had an appointment to see on that faithful day.

"You are welcome Mr Obodom." The officer was the one addressing him. "It is not actually intended to be a very long discussion. "The special assistance to the president on security affairs is also here with me. It was on the occasion of his security information that we have invited you. We are hopeful that the security concern warranting your invitation can easily be resolved to the benefit of us all and the nation at large.

They all shook hands even as he wondered the manner of security concern that warranted his invitation. He also wondered what he had done or did not do that occasioned the special assistance to the president getting a report on him. He immediately expressed his concern.

"I was surprised when I was visited this morning by some security personnel on the account of this invitation. I am even more surprised and confused too at what I just heard. I will appreciate a clarification. I really do not know of any action or inaction of mine that could have qualified the description of security concern. May be there must be a mix up of identity."

"Hahaha," laughed the Personal Assistance to the President.

"No, my dear friend there is no identity mix up. You delivered some speech to some university students to mark the commencement of their manifesto day. We do not know the exact content of the speech or what other actions you took earlier or after the speech that had incited and agitated the student body of the country and indeed the youths. Since after that, there had been numerous other cases of incitement most referencing you.

"The presidency is not happy at these events. Perhaps there could be a way of remedying what you have started. No one knows better than you what you did that has earned you so much respect of the youths to the extent that you have such cult-like followership in the country. I decided to take up this personally. We could factor out some sort of solution together.

"We would be meeting again. I want you, however to go and personally deliberate on this our discussion before our next meeting. Here is my complementary card. It will grant you a VIP entrance when you are invited for another discussion.

"You will be immediately returned to your house. I do not expect any immediate response from you at the moment. Have a wonderful day."

The two stood to leave indicating that they have nothing more to discuss with him at the moment. The door was barely shut when it opened again and Sergeant Irabo was in to usher him out.

He was at a loss on how to interpret his interaction with them. There was however no doubt in his mind that the meeting and the discussion held was intended to serve as a warning to him. It beat his imagination wondering what he had done wrong.

'What on earth was offensive about the talk he delivered to the students?' He was in deep thought even as he followed Irabor out of the office. He was still in thought when the vehicle stopped in front of his house. This time, it was just one vehicle that took him back. Perhaps they have seen and rightly too that there was no need of sending 2 vehicles and 6 officers to come and invite him for discussions or would he say instruction.

He opened his door and entered. The letter he had dropped for Barrister Nasser was still where he left it. He picked it and made his way to a seat, dropping the letter on the centre table in front of him. He was still unable to make out anything with his scamper with the security officers. It was unimaginable that his interaction with the students could be interpreted to incitement against the security of the state.

The coming of Nasser at that point brought him back to normalcy. Good that he came to rescue him from the distressful situation and perhaps help interpret what exactly Sergeant Irabo meant by classing his talk to the students' union body as incisive.

"Welcome Nasser, you came at the very right time. You will help me resolve an issue that just developed." He handed him the letter he had earlier left for him before proceeding with the security officers.

"What does this mean? - 2 vehicles with 6 security officers came to invite me 10:17hrs to their secretariat for security discussions. Don't really understand what for. The only clew I have of their identification is Sergeant Irabor, the particular officer that came to the door." Nasser asked reading out the content of the letter.

"What exactly do you mean by this letter? I can also see that the letter was addressed to me and it is in your hand writing." He probed further.

"Indeed I wrote the letter. As it clearly stated, 6 security personnel came this morning at about 10:17hours requesting that I follow them to their secretariat for security discussions. I don't understand what they meant as at the time they came and still do not understand what it all meant even after honouring their invitation.

"I was made to understand that my talk to the students before their manifesto day is of concern to the presidency. They claim that my talk had agitated and incited the students and all the youths of the country. This beats my imagination because I do not see how telling the youths to be responsive citizens can be adjudged as incisive. They did not stop there, I was asked to find a way to pacify the youths. I am to think about it to find a way to remedy the situation. I am expected for a second meeting by which time I am supposed to have thought out something. Tell me now, what am I to do?"

"Obodom, the invitation is supposed to act as a warning to you. I don't think anything will happen if you are seen not doing anything again. However if there is a repeat of such actions like the talk you had with the students it could be dangerous. These politicians are dangerous. They are capable of committing any atrocity to gain and remain in power. My advice to you now is that you apply caution in all you do."

"This actually is strange as well as funny. What exactly have I done wrong? If there is anything I have done wrong, I will immediately desist from it. If however my wrong doing was that I challenged the youths of this nation to do what is right for them. If my wrong is letting the youth know that they are stakeholders in the project called Nigeria. If indeed my wrong is wakening the consciousness of the youths to get involved in creating a better future not only for them but for the generation yet to be born. I want to be wrong and I will continue to be wrong. It is an oat I have sworn to honour my mothers.

"Nasser, you have known me for quite some time now and know my background very well. Will the evil that befell my late mother be allowed to thrive? Look at Osayiwmense and his mother. Does their condition suggest our society is working? There are numerous others like them that are wallowing in suffering and anguish and our political leadership is virtually doing nothing to change their situation?

"Are the youths supposed to relax under such situations? In fact if the citizenry of this country know their right, they would have continuously challenged their leaders to performance. The only thing I can do which is actually quite minimal is to wake up the youths to reject the gruesome future awaiting them. What is the wrong in doing that?"

"I perfectly understand you. Do not misunderstand me. I will never hinder your contribution to the society. My advice is for you to exercise caution but not to stop. You have to be tactful and careful in whatever you do. Remember that if you are dead no one will even do what you are doing no matter how small you think it is. I need you to be alive to continue or do you not understand that?"

"So, what exactly should I do?"

"You simply have to play along. One way or the other the invitation of the security personnel and involvement of the Personal Assistant to the President has to be made public subtly. When it becomes public knowledge that you had some chat with them on the account of your talk to the university students, they will become liable if any harm befalls you. At least they will be vicariously liable if they still have conscience at all. My worry however is how that can be effectively done without putting you to danger in the first place.

"Were you told when your next invitation with them will be?"

"No specific date was mentioned. All that I know is that I will be invited when next I am wanted. By the way why do you ask?"

"I am thinking of something. I think it will work"?

"What will work?"

"There is a Journalist I know working with Satellite Cable Network Television. He is one of the accredited Journalists covering the Presidential Villa. He will do the work."

"Which work? I still do not get it."

"I will discuss with him in advance and give him a dossier of you prepared in line with the information we want to get to the public. Of course, he has to know things about you. The information about you has to be true as to who you are; how you look; your outlook in life; and how you have been championing the reawakening of the patriotism of the youth in the era of nation building. When the invitation for a revisit comes, I will also make him aware and have him also on ground to interview you and telecast same.

"I know him quite well and know that he stands for justice and fairness. The only thing he will be expecting from me will be to be absolutely open in all things so that he can weigh his risks. I bet you, he may even have a better guide.

"Much as you are causing some wave of positive uprising you are still a small fry." He gave Obodom a cynical look.

"You know that I am not seeking popularity. I am not a politician whose popularity and acceptance is imminent for him to be elected into any position." He responded with a wry smile to humour his friend. He was now beginning to get his idea and is appreciative of his smartness.

"Nasser, I wonder why you are not even a politician. You are smarter than all those dumb fools that are governing the affairs of our nation."

"Don't go there my friend. You know I am not cut out for politics."

"That is exactly why things are going wrong. Those that can deliver don't get involved and those that get involved have nothing to offer. You really have to give it a thought."

"Ok. Let us discuss that another day. Our concern today is to figure out how we can keep you better secured even as you continue your crusade on nation building and reformation of the society at large.

"Remember that I said you are still a small fry. I mean no insult. What they are trying to do is to put off the flickering light before it turns into a mighty inferno. If you are more generally known and your message accepted in the society it becomes more dangerous for them to harm you. I have to work with this journalist and some others in other media houses to push you to lime light. You have to learn to be a celebrity my friend. The dangerous period therefore happens to be this period required to get you known to Nigerians for the good you are doing.

"I really have to work fast on this before your second invitation. In the time being, I advise you document all your movements and activities in a diary or sort of a log. Always keep someone abreast of what you intend to do. I leave you to figure out what to do on this. Immediately I leave, I will try to establish contact with the journalist."

TEN

•••••••••••••••••••••••••••••••

It took almost a week before Nasser was able to get in touch with the journalist, Ibifubara Pepple. Thankfully enough, Obodom have not received any invitation from anyone. When it was proving difficult for him to locate him Obodom had thought of jettisoning the idea completely.

"I really think we had over reacted to the whole matter. Maybe nothing bad was actually intended." Obodom tried discouraging Nasser.

"My exposure as a legal practitioner had thought me quite a lot", Nasser would not let him put off his plans. "The build-up of crime has numerous ways and such ways are mostly unusual. Crime does not tow the route of normalcy. If that was the case a lot of crimes would have been nipped in the bud. We would not lose anything by taking the precaution I advised."

Ibifubara patiently listened to what Nasser had to tell him looking around uncomfortably.

"Is anything wrong?" He asked him.

"Nothing that I can say for now, however, we have to work out something and somewhere more private. As an accredited journalist in the Presidential Villa, I can without being told tell you that it is important to those security details what I do; where I go and who I meet. The information you are giving seems to be a major journalistic scoop. I do not need to be warned by anyone to be careful. I know without being told what I am up to. I have observed other workers at the Presidential Villa being monitored and I don't expect my case to be any different.

"I appreciate the dossier on your friend that you have prepared but do not bring anything out here. Let us meet at Everyday Emporium Shopping Complex's snacks shop. Make sure you come with the month's publication of Lotus magazine. Put the profile inside your copy of the Magazine. We will discuss when we meet there.

"Come straight to the snack's shop at about 8:15pm. Your friend should also come though separately about same time. You will find me seated when you arrive. I will want to be acquainted with him prior to his invitation that you talked about at the Presidential Villa. Let me know if there is any further explanation you need. I will be leaving in the next 3 minutes if there is none."

"I read you loud and clear Sir," responded Nasser with a smile.

"I have learnt to be careful my friend. Since after the death of my close colleague who was at the nick of publishing an investigative expose he had on a drug trafficking network. He was sent a letter bomb that detonated when he wanted to open it. Since then I had learnt to be diligent and careful. See you later today as we have agreed."

Nasser's next move was to immediately contact Obodom to inform him of the arrangement that had been made later in the day.

"I guess by the time I am done with you, I will be awarded a degree in espionage." He jested with him after he had briefed him of everything. "I didn't know that one has to be this careful working as a journalist. Is this the way it is round the world or is this peculiar to Nigeria?" He further asked.

"I don't think it will ever be different anywhere. When you handle sensitive information, there is no need waiting to be told that you are working the path of danger. It is natural that perpetrators will make every effort to cover their evil shenanigans in the society. They will want to present themselves as clean personalities to the general public. Why are crimes not committed in the open? Why do criminals operate using mask or trade their businesses where they are not known. It is simply the same reasoning that informs all that. They are eager to cover up the evil misdeeds.

"Grow up my dear friend. You are going to become a celebrity very soon. Better be wise. Remember to be at the Everyday Emporium Shopping Complex's snacks shop as at when I told you. I had better start going. Who knows, may be in the immediate future I have to be careful seeing you too. Can you imagine that?"

Much as Obodom jested over the entire thing it was actually getting him thoughtful. It dawned on him that life has so much in its stock. It is stockpiled with its good, bad and ugly. He wondered if one can ever be too careful with all he had witnessed and seen in life. If there is anything he wanted, it was a simple quiet life. A life that he would be down to earth having no need of being so cautious in all that he has to do.

He wondered what use it was to anyone to harm him. If that is what was needed to be within the corridors of power and governance, he would never want to have anything to do with it. However, it was not by his conscious decision that he got involved. The memory of his late mother is a lesson that when everyone does nothing, things keep getting out of hand. To do nothing in the face of numerous things to do to get the society better was like succumbing to the vagaries of nature and as such it was like abandoning the weaker ones of the society at the mercy of evil ones. The political class whose duty it was to protect the weak have become their predators.

'Who will fight for them? Who will protect them? There was none to protect my mother, not even her own guardian. For this reason she was robbed and raped. As a minor, she suffered great deprivation as she bore her pregnancy without any medical care until delivery. No one was there for her. Now it is my opportunity to be there for someone. I would not allow anyone to stop me. Yes, there may be great threat to my life but I would not give up. I know that if it pleases the Almighty God he will keep me safe to fight on.' He thought to himself.

"Oh! My dear Lord, you know I really cannot boast of any personal defences except You protect me. Help me dear God and keep me safe to contribute the little that I can." He prayed out aloud in all earnest to God.

At Everyday Emporium Shopping Complex, Nasser was already there and a man was with him on a table. He could safely presume he was the journalist and moved to sit with them.

"Good Evening." He greeted as he sat opposite Nasser. "I am Obodom Agozie. I suppose you are Ibifubara Pepple?"

"Yes. Good evening Obodom. I have heard of you and most importantly now we know ourselves. Good to meet you."

"Good to meet you."

"Well, I will appreciate to hear from you directly, your experience with the security officers on one hand and your famous speech to the students that got the government agitated. I really would want to know exactly what transpired that got the presidency feel so threatened as to send 6 security officers looking for you."

Obodom told his story once again, trying not to miss out anything of significance while Nasser and Ibifubara listened intently. Ibifubara was also taking some notes as he listened nodding his head intermittently as if to urge him on. Not to look too out of place, they had also made some order of snacks and drinks like others around them.

"Please see if you can get me a recording of your speech at the university. I am going to read your profile that Nasser has prepared in the comfort of my home. Let him have the recording of your address when you get it. He will know how to get it to me. I have seen you well enough and will easily identify you whenever you get your second invitation to visit the Presidential Villa. It goes without saying that the information should immediately be given to me when that happens.

"I will work out my manner of ensuring that Nasser and I can easily get in touch with one another. I do not think we have any reason to meet again. Since you are the hounded, it is important that you keep low and that you are more careful. My knowledge of the powers-that-be and politicians is that they are capable of anything. When I say anything, I am not mincing words, I mean it in reality.

"For the fact that those security officers exercise even the slightest hunch that they are protecting the interest of their principal, they can eliminate anybody for that matter. Sometimes they do that without their principals even having an inkling of what they are doing. I am not telling you this to scare you, these are facts. Be careful while we work this out for the good of the society we have found ourselves."

Obodom wanted to say something but rather thought it better not to. Somehow, he still feels that the entire matter was being over exaggerated. Whatever the situation however he needed not being told that it was better to tow the path of caution. There was nothing to lose being careful. He was also aware that there must be some sense of urgency in getting the recording of his address to the students' body of the university.

'Thank God, I have kept in touch with Mubo, the students' union outgoing President.' He thought to himself. He was not very sure that they record their activities however; he had already decided that he was going to see her the next day.

When he remembered that he had been cautioned to be careful, he wondered whether he would ever be careful enough. Nothing displeased him more than living a regimental life. It was for the same reason that he was sure he was never going to be able to serve in police not to talk of any of the armed forces. If that was how his freedom will go then he was in for a very rough time.

As part of exercising caution, he decided to alter his dressing in a way that will not immediately give him up. He got himself sun glasses and a faze cap. He knew that the easiest way to get her would be by going to the students' union secretariat. However, he decided to avoid the place but rather to put a call to the Union's office.

"Good morning. This is students' union office, how may I help you?" A lady responded to the call.

He had really not thought through on how to approach the situation and was a bit lost on what to respond.

"Good morning." He greeted her before an idea flashed into his mind. "Please bear with me if I am a bit secretive. It is important I speak to Mubo Awoyemi. I have information to share with her. In order not to leave you in much doubt, I am not a student. I am not expecting that she must certainly be in the office so you can help by telling me when to repeat my call to speak with her."

"Bear with me Sir, your request is a little awkward to me. I hope you are not expecting her to jump at the prospect of her being eager to speak to a strange caller."

"Of course not, we know ourselves well enough. It is just that it's neither safe nor reasonable in the prevailing circumstances not to conceal my identity from her. Just try to understand. Just create the enablement for me to talk with her. I know that she will oblige me. She is not expecting me though but I am certain she will oblige me. If only you will let her know of my discussion with you let me be the loser if she refuses."

"If you say so, I advise you call again in the next ten to fifteen minutes." She responded before she ended the call.

He did not have to call. It was not up to 8 minutes after their discussion that his phone rang and it was a call from the student union's phone number that he had just called. Graciously enough, it was Mubo Awoyemi on the other side of the phone. You can't ever miss the voice. It was as elegant as the day he heard her first.

"Good morning, this is Mubo Awoyemi speaking."

Good morning Mubo, it is me Obodom Agozie. Thank you for returning my call. You can be sure you did not disappoint me; I was actually expecting you would respond to my call. Please I have reason to see you immediately without the prying eyes of anyone today. It is really not going to take long but it is important and urgent, if you pardon my saying so."

"Oh! It is you. I had really wondered who it was and curious also what it is all about. Where are you now?"

"I am at the newspaper stand near the students' centre. Perhaps you can guide me to another area with some serenity."

"Look to your right from where you are. You will see the sports building. Walk into it and wait there. I will join you within five minutes of your getting there."

It was easy to identify the sports building and he bought a newspaper and made his way to the building. He had virtually sat down when he sighted her coming.

"Good morning Mr Obodom. I must confess I am a little curious at your visit and the manner of it. If my guess is right, however, it must not be unconnected with your earlier visit. So let me know how correct my guess is."

It was his turn to get curious. He was therefore visibly agitated when he spoke.

"By this you mean that you are actually aware why I am here? I cannot believe this."

"Well it is not actually difficult for me to figure things out. The only thing that had made me to know you was our students' union politics. You had come to deliver a talk to us to commence our manifesto night. The event took a shape and nature of its own. The first indication I had about this was my invitation by the Vice Chancellor to his office about a week after the event. He enquired about the invited speaker who happened to be you. Specifically, he was seeking to know who you were and how I got to be acquainted with you.

"I did explain to him the circumstances of our meeting and how you indicated your interest to speak to our students of which I didn't see anything wrong with. I went further to acquaint him with the content of your presentation and explained further to him that it was nothing injurious to the school. So I tried based on this my understanding to find out why he is interested in who speaks to the student.

"He smiled and informed me that nothing of our activity affected the institution. His sudden interest was only because some security personnel were interested and wanted to know. In fact it was through them that he realized we had an invited guest for the event.

"When I asserted that your discussion should not worry them for any reason. He affirmed that he told them same but informed me that they may be coming to me for a chat. Of course I found that really ridiculous. I did not as I said see the reason why they should be interested in your presentation for that matter. If anything they are supposed to be appreciative of your effort to make the youths of this country become more responsive citizens. Ridiculous however as I thought the matter to be it did not stop them from coming to me for some discussion. I did not also mince words in telling them my views about the whole thing and even warning them that they should desist from interfering in the affairs of our students and I meant my warning to them. The students of this great institution will resist any effort from any angle or quarters to intimidate them into docility.

"So tell me, have the Security personnel visited you? In fact, tell me why you are here. Have anyone told you of my intension to also invite you for the inaugural lecture of the new students' union executives and you have come to refuse the invitation?"

Obodom burst out into a hearty laugh. Speaking in between his laugh he said;

"What you prophesied about my visitation by the security personnel is correct. The only thing however is that I am not aware of your intended invitation. So I have not come to reject any invitation. My visit rather is to make effort to get the nation know that they are after me because of the discussions I had with you students. By doing this, it is intended that they will desist from any evil machinations which I fear they may progress to if not deterred.

"I have therefore come to solicit for help from you."

"You don't have to hesitate. How can I be of help to you?"

"I have a Journalist acquaintance who wants to bring my presentation to your union into public knowledge. He solicited for audio-visual recording of the event if there is any. That is why I have come hopeful that I can get one from you."

Mubo was thoughtful for a while before she spoke.

"I really cannot say for sure that there is any. There is however a member of the union's parliament who also is among the campus journalists. I know he records most of the events that occur in the institution from which he normally extracts whatever he deem well enough for his journalistic flair.

"I will try without appearing to be desperate see if he has any and how I can get a copy of it. What I am thinking of now is to leverage on his knowledge of the chat I had with the security personnel and demand that I really want to have a review of the event from his recording." She suddenly stopped talking.

"No", she continued after a while. "It is not absolutely correct for me to divulge his material to a third party without his permission. I will let him know why I need it and persuade him to make out a copy for the purpose."

He cannot afford to be less agreeable with her on that. 'Whatever is worth doing is worth doing right,' he thought.

"Please, I will advise you come again tomorrow by the same time. I will try to conclude with him today. Whatever be the outcome you will know by the time you visit tomorrow. And now that you know of my intention to invite you in the future, precisely in about a fortnight, start preparing your presentation from now."

"You know that I will not waste any opportunity to energize the youths to a positive force that will take over the leadership of this country in the future. I will try my best not to disappoint you and the nation when the time comes. I will take my leave now."

As he set to go, his mind was also set to even be more assertive in his coming presentation to the students' body. There was also no doubt in his mind that there was need to review future plans with Nasser and Ibifubara especially as regards the future presentation to the union. He immediately set himself to arrange another meeting of the three of them as soon as possible.

ELEVEN

• •

The pace of things eventually got faster. The three, Obodom, Nasser and Ibifubara held there meeting as had been planned by Obodom. They were unanimous in their agreement that Obodom should honour the invitation by the students' union body. It was equally agreed among them that the coming event will be covered fully by another journalist that Ibifubara would send. He would not personally attend for the reason that he would defeat their purpose if it was seen that it was him alone that was projecting Obodom. That would also jeopardise his accreditation to the Presidential Villa. He would not want to lose that opportunity as a journalist. It would not be in his interest also to do that.

Their sole wish at the end of the meeting was that Obodom would be lucky to get a recording of his previous presentation to the students. Everything also suggests a better future not just for the youths but for the entire country. One way or the other, they envisaged that more is required to be done. There was also no doubt in any of their minds that caution is of essence.

When Obodom went back to see Mubo, he was only hopeful that her discussion with the member of the parliament of the students' union would be eventful. Therefore he observed her countenance as she approached him even as they exchanged pleasantries.

"Good morning Mubo."

"Good morning. How has your day been?"

"Should I count myself lucky?" He asked directly as he was not able to discern from her countenance if she succeeded.

"You are," she responded smiling. "One thing with the Nigerian youths is that they want the progress of this country more than any other person. The moment I explained to him the reason for the request he never minded parting with his recording. I however insisted that what would be better to do was to reproduce a copy which I now recorded in a flash drive."

"Mubo, quite seriously you have great things to do for this country. I would not like you to just stop at being the president of your students' union. You must continue beyond that. You know, if you ask yourself the question, are things going on wrongly in the country because we lack good people?" He asked rhetorically.

"No of course," he continued, "it is simply because the good ones do not offer themselves for service to the nation building on one hand. On the other, the good ones are quite docile and complacent. As far as they are concerned whoever gets the position of leadership was put there by God. The parlance of politicking is left for those that are bereft of any goodness. So what should we expect from such people if not calamity.

"We have to do something to salvage the situation and urgently too. Why the sense of urgency. When we increase the level of awareness of the greater percentage of the populace and them in turn also by the manner of their living positively affect others then there is hope. If however it does not happen that way we are in for trouble. I know it because there is always a limit to the extent of suffering the people are willing to bear. If it gets to that extent the people assume unbearable, the next thing becomes a revolution."

"I rather wish that the revolution will come immediately," Mubo interjected.

"The revolution I see, if it will come will be utterly bloody. It will be extremely bloody and catastrophic. The arrow head will be the absolutely deprived members of the society. Look at things as they are currently. There are numerous street urchins. They have no family affiliation or any emotional attachment to anybody. They are poor and hungry. There is no one that cares for them. These kids are growing up with bitterness against the elites and the political leadership of the nation.

"Mind you, this has not erased their knowledge of the fact that they are from this country. You cannot deny them that fact. Gradually they are growing up to become adults. By their actions, they are making serious demands that no one is attending to. They are also asking the same questions that most of the oppressed citizens are asking. Questions like; 'why those that make no efforts are rewarded better than others? What are the political leaders and elites of the country doing for the citizens? Is it worth it trusting our lives in the hands of people who care less about our wellbeing?'

"I think it was late Johann Goethe, 1749 to 1832 who said – 'No revolution is the fault of the people but the fault of the government.' Like I said a revolution is fast approaching. The mostly dehumanized and downtrodden populace, who currently are like beggars and powerless are sick and fed up of begging in their country. They are aware that their country is blessed with numerous resources. They find no justifiable reason why they should continue to beg. They are aware of nations that hitherto were bestowed with nothing who are ruling the world because of the quality leadership they have. They are equally aware that many nations who depended on the country to succeed in the past have now overtaken the country. They wonder why that should be and they get no satisfactory answer.

"These people are now demanding for their own share of 'the national cake.' They begged for their share politely and gently but got nothing. They look around and are witnessing the sharing of the same cake and none is getting to them. They see others getting more than their proportionate share, yet not even the crumps are allowed to get to them. They witnessed a few that took up arms to forcefully get a piece of the action and were baffled that even they got a lot more than they bargained for. It had become obvious to them that he that fights gets settled to keep quiet and make no further noise. They are no longer content with keeping quiet anymore.

"Mubo, you must see this revolution that I am seeing. You must also understand why I said it is going to be extremely violent and bloody. I will do this by creating a scenario for you. Imagine you drove your car to a place and you met a foe who you despise so much. Tell me Mubo, would you take up a stone and smash the windscreen of his car?" He asked rhetorically.

"No! You will not." He continued, "Why? Of course, he that lives in a glass house does not throw stones. If you smash his windscreen, he can easily get even with you by smashing yours also. Do you understand now what I mean? These people that would revolt have absolutely nothing to lose. No assets; I repeat absolutely nothing to lose. It would be so difficult for the government to contend with them. They would be worse than these terrorists we are all hearing about.

"I can go on and on to make you see reason why it is urgent and in everyone's interest that people like you should get involved. Please think about this seriously." He further advised as he set to go.

Mubo was as if transfixed to the spot even as she watched him depart. He was so very passionate about the affairs of the country. There he was thinking that she should get involved, but she had her own thoughts too. She had never in her life seen or read about anyone that was that passionate for anything. He was always looking up to other people to do the job. It was he however that was best soothed for this liberation that he so passionately advocates for.

She kept her eyes on him even as she ravished in her thinking of what exactly she could do. Each time she heard him speak, it often left her dizzy with this enthusiastic urge to do something for the good of the country. She kept looking until distance pickled him out of view and she made her way back to the student union office.

It was that same day that she made the resolute decision.

'I will do whatever is possible to propel this man to the leadership of this nation. There is no way such a person with this great amount of passion for the good of the nation will be in existence and this nation will be wallowing under the clutches of mediocrity. I will reach out to all other student body to get him involved in their programme. This I must do.' She resolved

Obodom himself did not leave without his own thinking. One thing that impressed him about Mubo was her gentile nature and humility. She has such a nature that people readily accept her person and is willing to support her in anything or venture. She can readily market any project no matter how difficult it may be.

'This is the greatest trait of leadership and that is what the nation needs at this point in time. I must find a way to get her interested in getting involved in the nation's politics. She may not immediately assume any position of leadership or authority but her impact will be positively felt by all. She has such an infectious personality that no one can resist.' He resolved as he made effort to deliver his recorded presentation to Nasser as was agreed in their last meeting.

He was not really very sure how that was going to assist Ibifubara. The relevance of whatever he was planning to do was also yet to be appreciated by him. He was indeed being distracted as far as he could tell and imagine. In any case he was happy he was able to secure the recorded speech and as soon as he was able to give it to Nasser, he would only worry about the invitation of the presidential security officers. When the time comes whatever happened then, he would take it up from there.

All that he had simply wanted out of life was a just and equitable life for all. A society that guaranteed the wellbeing of all her citizens would just be it. Everyone thereafter would just have followed his or her passion. Unfortunately, the human race can never be content with these ideals. If things were simply like that there would not have been Osayiwmense and the mother to attend to. Perhaps it would not have even mattered to him whatever was happening in the society. Indeed it was the imperfection of the society that created the circumstances of his birth. That in turn created the concern in him of the need for a better society. Whether he would be able to impact on the society to the extent of his choice remained for him to see.

As days passed by it was dawning on him that it was not as easy as he had supposed. He had never envisaged that anyone would see his intensions and actions as offending. His anticipation was that the society and indeed the government would be more supportive. Rather than that he was rather looking for help on how to safeguard himself from the same government. He was rather wasting time on personal security than looking for things to do to make the lot of the common man better.

It was almost night time before he was able to meet Nasser and handed over to him the recorded speech. They were both exhausted by their activities of the day and were more concerned about retiring for the day. Their discussions were quite brief and they parted.

TWELVE

●●●●●●●●●●●●●●●●●●●●●●●●●●●●●

Ibifubara sat watching and listening to the recording of the speech of Obodom Agozie to the students that had just received from Nasser. He had watched and listened to the video thrice. By now he had almost memorized every statement and action on it. There was nothing really in it that should be of any concern to anybody of right conscience. Indeed he found it ridiculous that the political leadership of the country would leave meaningful things they were supposed to do and be looking for an innocent citizen of the country that had committed no crime against the state.

'I will make sure that they are even more disturbed by the time I am done with the interview. I will so ridicule them that they will realize the need to live up to their governmental responsibility.' He was all in thought and imagination on how best he was to handle the entire thing. Also on his mind was the issue of finding the right journalist that will attend to Obodom's address during the inauguration of the new student union executive and through which media it was to be broadcast for maximum effect and result.

On his diary he scribbled questions that will be best to ask Obodom during the interview. His own interview will be broadcast on Satellite Cable Network Television where he works. He has to package it very well to be of no harm to his organisation. That will be his first huddle. He would not want anything that will result to his organization losing prominence and recognition.

His only discomfiture then was that of waiting indefinitely for Obodom's invitation by the presidential Villa security officials. He would not want that when the invitation was eventually made there will be some unforeseen hick up. Earnestly he hoped that nothing of the sort would happen. He also was hopeful that the invitation will not be jettisoned completely by them.

In any case, he had no choice but to wait and that was exactly what he set himself to do. That in itself was in a way welcome by him. As time passed by, he developed new strategy with which to handle the issue. He was also getting new supportive materials that will enhance the potency of the interview itself in addressing the social vices of the nation.

Everyone had been a victim of the leadership anomaly of the country. The loss may not be directly though, but there was no doubt in his mind that all had lost one way or the other. A nation where things are working as it should be is normally to the betterment of the entire citizenry. He recounted bitterly the death of Carol, her cousin's baby after she had battled childlessness for about 8 years. There was no functional incubator in the hospital. The one there had started to malfunction. There was a competent Biomedical Engineer under the employ of the hospital who was ready and had all it required to fix it but was not allowed by the medical director.

It was after the incidence that he petitioned the Medical Director on the matter to the medical council. His petition did not get to its destination before he was expelled from work. The Medical Director got wind of the petition and leveraged on his intimacy to the Minister of health made sure it never got to the Council before the Biomedical Engineer was relieved of his job.

He made effort then to approach him to provide him more information on the matter for him to take it up within the press and electronic media. The man was no longer much interested in following up the matter. He secured admission abroad, left the country to further his studies.

'God knows what had become of the man,' he thought bitterly. Somehow he became apprehensive and hoped that Obodom would not become a victim in his effort to contribute to the betterment of his dear country. It was only time that will tell but the time was not known. He ardently prayed that for the very sake of the suffering populace those things would turn for the better.

Obodom was also getting bored of waiting. If there was anything he would not want to happen it was for the inauguration day to approach without the expected invitation to the Presidential Villa. He was aware that would mess up a lot for him and may impede the success of Nasser and Ibifubara to achieve their effort in ensuring that the public is aware of the effort of the state to use the tax payers' money to suppress, intimidate and who knows assassinate him.

He shook in fear as he thought about himself being assassinated. 'Would anybody really go to that extent?' He asked no one in particular. If things like that does not happen there would not have been the basis for Nasser and Ibifubara to harbour such fear of its happening which was the reason for all the effort that was being made to get it to the knowledge of the public.

As he approached his house, however he saw a black vehicle parked a couple of houses before his. He noticed that the driver of the vehicle pointed at him before it occurred to him that it was one of those vehicles that had come earlier to pick him up the first time. When the taxi that brought him stopped finally, he also noticed that the second black car was parked by the building after his house. Something made him feel the first vehicle he had seen will come after him but he however did not look back. He wanted to pretend he was not aware they were there.

It also looked funny to him that they would take the pains to come after him in like manner again. His expectation and that of Nasser and Ibifubara was that they would send him a letter inviting him on a particular date or at least call him on phone to book an appointment. He wondered what gave them the impression that he had nothing doing other than to follow them every time they come for him. That actually was the main reason of his unhappiness; he was scared he would not have the opportunity to get in touch with his lawyer and friend Nasser. 'How was he going to alert him or Ibifubara for that matter that they had taken him without any notice?' It all meant that all their plans had been truncated. 'Will that not mean perhaps that they are aware of their plans in the first instance?' He was seriously worried. There was actually nothing he could do than to allow things to play out on its own. Whatever happened they would try and see what they can make out of it.

As he fiddled and brought out his house key, he made every effort to maintain his composure. The car that was ahead remained where it was but the one behind had driven up and parked in front of his house.

Captain Irabor walked up to him even before he could open his door.

"Good evening Mr Obodom." He greeted politely not minding their impolite visit.

'Good evening Captain Irabor. He responded. "I was expecting an invitation if you require me and not another visit. At least you attested to that the last time."

It appeared Irabor was taken aback by his direct confrontation on the matter. His speech stuttered as he spoke further.

"It is not that it cannot be done. It is just that this was decided instantaneously."

"So what is the visit about this time? Is it to have another discussion as if I have no use of my time or that someone else decides for me how my time is to be used?"

He was visibly angry and that was not lost on Irabor. His anger was greatly because things were bound to deviate from their intended plans.

'How was he to get in touch with either Nasser or Ibifubara to acquaint them with the new development?' He was indeed bitter to imagine that all effort made to catch in on this invitation had been wasted. He would now visit presidential Villa without Ibifubara knowing about it. 'This will imply that there would no longer be any interview,' He was in an apprehensive fear. 'Could it be that they are privy of our plans and intensions already and the sudden invitation was actually to thwart everything? They have indeed dealt us a lethal blow if this is the case,' he thought regretfully. He felt both stupid and foolish to have spent all those times planning and not being able eventually to achieve anything of his plan. When he got into his house to drop off the few things that were with him, he also scribbled down some note for Nasser.

'They have come to pick me up. No time to get across to you or Ibifubara.'

He resolved to allow things take their cause naturally. There was nothing he could do anymore. 'Whatever happens now so be it,' he resolved further and got himself ready to follow them. After everything he would explain to Ibifubara and Nasser what happened. If there be anything that could be done to remedy the situation they would then decide. If on the other hand there was nothing that could be done they would also allow it as such and decide on an alternative action. 'May be these men are not really dumb as most people take them to be.' He grinned to himself in self-surrender as he followed them to their car.

The journey to their secretariat was faster this time around or so it appeared to him. Everything was still the same as it was in the office. He waited in anticipation of what they were going to tell him this time around.

It was also the same persons he met during his last visit that came to see him. He remembered the chubby Special Assistance to the President on security matters.

"Mr Obodom my friend, we are meeting again. You are quite the luckiest man I have ever seen. I cannot imagine that His Excellency rather than see you for the threat you pose for his political future is taking you as a friend. Anyway, that depends a lot on if you accept his friendship or rebuff it. So tell me Obodom are you a friend or foe?"

It was his time to be surprised. There was nothing he could make out from his proposition. 'What indeed is he saying?' He was wondering to himself and did not hesitate to let him know.

"Honestly," He paused trying to figure out his name.

"Ndifreke, I am Ndifreke."

"Ndifreke, I honestly do not understand you. There is no way I can be a foe to my President. I have not done anything to suggest any hostility to him. It is in my interest that he succeeds as I envisage not just me but every citizen of our country will want him to succeed." He clearly asserted his position to make it clear to him that it was not his intension to be confrontational to anyone talk less of the President himself.

"Well, his Excellency would want you to do something for him. He has rightly noted your passion for the youth of the country. He also desires to involve the youth more in his administration. To put matters straight to you, he wants to set up a governmental committee to investigate the restiveness of the youths and recommend ways of resolving it. He would want you to head the committee. So are you prepared and ready to render your services in that capacity?"

This was not what he was expecting when he came here. How can security attaché to the President call him here for someone to make a proposal to him of the head of a governmental committee? What exactly recommends him for such a position? Is the offer borne out of good intention or is it all a trap? He was simply confused. He looked around the office as if he was assessing it for a possible way of escape.

"I really do not know what to say or answer you," he started to say but kept quiet.

"Go ahead," Ndifreke prodded him on. "Are you sure you understand what it means that the President is making you such an offer?"

"I do surely understand that aspect of your statement. How would you explain that I am invited by the security attaché of the president for questioning and all I ended up getting is an offer to head a governmental committee? What qualifies me for such an appointment? Mr Ndifreke, I do not see myself as cut out for such position in as much as I will like to see the youths get positively involved in the affairs of this country. I repeat myself, positively involved in the affairs of this country.

"As for me assuming any political appointment no that cannot be. That however, is not to say that I am or would be a foe of the president. Please don't take it in that light."

"Ok." He answered abruptly and got up.

"I will find a way to communicate to the President that you refused his offer. I don't think he is going to like that."

As he stood to go the other also stood and Obodom realized his company was no longer required. He also stood up and immediately Irabor stepped in to usher him out.

He led him outside the premises and excused himself that he has some urgent assignment and hoped he would be able to find his way easily back to his house.

He had virtually stepped out of the gate when he saw Ibifubara stepping towards him with a microphone. Another man at that instance appeared almost out of the dark with a camera taking a good view of him with his back to the gate as barrage of questions started. He made great effort to hide his surprise and acted ignorant of knowledge of him.

"Mr Obodom, you spoke once at a university event which if you permit me to use the term went viral, what had brought you to the Presidential Villa?"

It took him time to pull himself together. There was no way he expected to see Ibifubara again. He could not help but imagine what really happened that made him to come. 'In any case that is an issue for another day' he thought within himself.

"Well, don't make me feel like a celebrity that I am not. I was actually invited by the security attaché to the Presidential villa for some discussion bordering on that talk I had with the students." He started to answer to the interview. He was cut in between the web coming out open or for the sake of the discussion he had with the security officers be reserved and conservative with his answers. Making situation worrisome was his uncertainty on whether he was answering Ibifubara well in line with his expectations or not. He lost the opportunity of benefitting from a pre session of how to answer the interview questions if he had had futuristic invitation. He only hoped that he would be able to get from his answers enough to have a good presentation.

"Can you come out more specific on your answer? Why would you be invited for discussions because you spoke to students? I would actually like to know how it mattered to the security personnel of the Presidential Villa."

"As you very well know, I am a civilian. I do not know how security matters are handled especially as it borders on ensuring adequate security for the nation. This is even more valid when you realize that it had to do with the presidency. They the security details of the presidency will be better informed with the security architecture of the nation. I will not like to answer that question on their behalf. One thing that I know however is that it is their opinion that my discussion with the students are offending to them. They will be in a better position to answer the question."

"I listened to your discussion with the students. As a matter of fact, it was the talk that interested me about you. You were passionate in your call on the youths to get involved in the matters of this country. I also believe it will serve the nation well if they will engage their youthful energy to address the issues of this country. I don't actually think that the presidency should feel disturbed by such a talk. Don't you have any idea no matter how remote, why they feel offended by your discussion with the students?"

"I would have told you if I know. It will not benefit me or anybody for that matter not to tell if I know why it would border the presidency. In any case, you are now my witness since you listened to what I told the students. I do also wish you have a recorded version so that you would replay it and convince yourself of the veracity of your opinion on this."

"We know how we get our information as journalists. We will legitimately get any information we want. It has been nice talking to you Mr Obodom Agozie."

'Has it really been nice indeed? Has it really gone the way you wanted it?' He wondered as they parted ways. It was still a wonder to him how he got a wind that he was taken by the security attaché to the Presidential Villa. Could it have been merely a coincidence that he was there to interview him? 'I will know eventually how it all happened,' he concluded.

He took a quick look around as if to find out if he was being monitored before he set to go home. If anything, he wanted to see Nasser immediately. However, he also knew that he had to be careful in doing that. It was just as he had to be careful over all things now. There was need however for him to get home first. He would start by verifying if Nasser had visited him and perhaps seen the letter he dropped for him.

He took a good look around his neighbourhood as the taxi took the last turn to enter his street. He smiled as he wondered if his neighbour had any inkling on what he was going through in the hands of the security officers. For all he knew they could have eliminated him if they had wanted without anyone being aware that anything was even going on. It was then understandable why some people often installed CCTV in and around their houses. He was filled with deep sense of insecurity. Somehow what he was going through was tantamount to harassment.

'Why would the government rather use the instrument of the state to intimidate and harass their citizens,' he wondered bitterly. As he saw that the letter for Nasser was no longer where he had kept it he was better relaxed. It all meant that he came not very long after he had gone with those security officers. In any case, he would arrange to see him. There were so many things they require to straighten out apart from his meeting with the security men.

Nasser was also on the look out for him. His initial surprise was to find out that Obodom has been apprehended by the security personnel from Presidential Villa. He had expected that as they informed earlier that Obodom would be required to go by himself on receipt of another invitation from them. It ought to have been clear to them that he would naturally honour their invitation. He was instantly curious. He had come to see Obodom over the progress of Osayiwmense's mother. He was surprised he was not at home then. While they had their discussion, he informed him that he would be at home. His surprise was abated when he opened the door to see the letter he had left for him.

Just as was the worry of Obodom himself when he was accosted by the security officers, he had wondered how the information could be passed to Ibifubara that he had been taken to the Presidential Villa security secretariat. Instantaneously he made up his mind to visit Ibifubara to acquaint him of the situation. Unfortunately he was not at home and there was no where he could possibly trace him to at that point in time. He could not help wondering as Obodom did if they were privy of their arrangement. "If that was not the case why the sudden change of plan?" He asked no one in particular.

Even as was the case with Obodom he equally relaxed himself to faith. Perhaps when he is back, they would re strategize. Whatever the case they would find a way. There must definitely be other ways to sort things out. They would not cease him there for the entire day,' he assured himself, 'definitely not.'

An eatery signage that stood ahead of him was what it took to remind him that he had barely had anything to eat that day. It was a welcome release that he strolled in. It took him little time deciding what to eat. It was more of the need to eat than the choice of what to eat. He thought of his activities for the day: how well Osayiwmense's mother was doing; Osayiwmense himself has been enrolled in a school. Obodom would be pleased to receive all these news. He has to wait however until he was back.

THIRTEEN

• •

"What am I seeing?" Nasser asked as the waiter dropped his order on the table.

"Sir, these are what you ordered. Please let me know if you had intended something different." She was perplexed by his question. She was the one that took his order and was sure of what he ordered. There was certainly no error in what she served him.

"Oh! Please pardon me. It is not about my order; it is the episode on the television." He clarified the waiter.

Being telecast on the programme 'events from the Villa' was an interview session of Obodom Agozie. 'Ibifubara, you are really worse than a spy,' he muted to himself. How was he able to track him? Who informed him of Obodom's invitation to the Presidential Villa? He took his mind off the unanswered questions to concentrate better on the interview.

"Mr Obodom, you spoke once at a university event which if you permit me to use the term went viral, what had brought you to the Presidential Villa?"

"Well, don't make me feel like a celebrity that I am not. I was actually invited by the security attaché to the Presidential villa for some discussion bordering on the talk I had with the students."

"Can you come out more specific on your answer? Why would you be invited for discussions because you spoke to students? I would actually like to know how it mattered to the security personnel of the Presidential Villa."

"As you very well know, I am a civilian. I do not know how security matters are handled especially as it borders on ensuring adequate security for the nation. This is even more valid when you realize that it had to do with the presidency. They the security details of the presidency will be better informed with the security architecture of the nation. I will not like to answer that question on their behalf. One thing that I know however is that it is their opinion that my discussion with the students are offending to them. They will be in a better position to answer the question."

"I listened to your discussion with the students. As a matter of fact, it was the talk that interested me about you. You were passionate in your call on the youths to get involved in the matters of this country. I also believe it will serve the nation well if they will engage their youthful energy to address the issues of this country. I don't actually think that the presidency should feel disturbed by such a talk. Don't you have any idea no matter how remote, why they feel offended by your discussion with the students?"

"I would have told you if I know. It will not benefit me or anybody for that matter not to tell if I know why it would border the presidency. In any case, you are now my witness since you listened to what I told the students. I do also wish you have a recorded version so that you would replay it and convince yourself of the veracity of your opinion on this."

"We know how we get our information as journalists. We will legitimately get any information we want. It has been nice talking to you Mr Obodom Agozie."

"Wonderful," said Nasser to no one in particular. He took a couple of bites of the food on his table which by them has turned cold, made his payment and was set to go.

"Is there anything wrong with the food?" asked the waiter. She was obviously disturbed wondering if he was not satisfied with their service.

"No, the food was very good. It is just that I had to go meet up with some urgent concerns."

"In that case, please give me a little time to arrange it for a take away."

"Good, I will wait. Thank you so very much. I am very pleased at your services."

She was indeed very good at her job and within 10 minutes she had it all packaged and delivered. 'How wonderful it would have been if everyone was this diligent on their job,' he thought as he tipped her and thanked her once more for her wonderful service.

His first point of call was Ibifubara. He was really very curious to find out how he was able to pull through this. He has always known how devoted and keen he was on his job. This notwithstanding, he was immensely impressed. He has indeed given up on his being able to get the interview he wanted with Obodom.

With the suddenness of the second visit, there was no way the interview would have been possible.

"Ibifubara my man," he applauded him on seeing him. "You are very good. How did you do it? How were you able to know he was coming to the Presidential Villa?"

"Ha! Ha! Ha!" He laughed loudly. "I love the complement. Thank you very much. However, we were simply lucky. You know we spy on one another in Presidential Villa. Some spy for the purposes of prosecution, if you permit me to say that while some, like me do so just to be on guard and avoid surprises. I really cannot afford any surprise.

"When I discovered the people that visited Obodom, I decided to keep a track on them my own way. That I did through their dispatcher. He somehow feels indebted to me for a favour I did him in the past. When as we were discussing about the performance of the President, I understood his displeasure at being used to intimidate the opposition I cached in on that by informing him of a young man I heard his people are tailing which is Obodom. I wanted to know what harm his speaking to the students of the university meant to the government. I informed him further that I see that as a big journalistic scoop for me if I can track the story as it unfolds.

"To my greatest surprise, he offered me more than what I bargained for. He assured me that he would keep me abreast of everything that is happening about the case. A day before their visitation to Obodom, he gave me the news of their intension though he was not certain of the time. I cared less of the time as I have knowledge of the day of need. I have laid siege for a story for 3 months so a day siege for the solution to the challenges of the problems of this country would not be too much for me.

"So it is now clear to you that I am not clairvoyant in anyway. Even Obodom was baffled when he saw me. He was not expecting me when I came but he is really smart. His answers to my questions were apt on point as will serve our purpose beautifully. I noted his bewilderment when he first saw me. Have you been in touch with him? He deserves commendation on his performance. If there was anything I was bordered about it was actually that the impromptu nature of my interview would put him in bad stand, but that was not the case. The only outstanding concern now is to find out why they seemed in a haste to call him up again.

"How are we going to meet? This may be the last time we are going to meet socially. I bet you that from now on there may be a closer monitoring of Obodom and his entire close associates. With regards to you there is nothing unusual as his lawyer. The only thing would be that you would assume the same level of monitoring as him. However my case is different. I have been guided in relating to you both to avoid cheap conclusions from our association. This would reduce the potency of any article I write on Obodom.

"So where and how are we to meet to know why he was invited and decide on how we progress from there?"

"If you don't mind, my suggestion will be that we meet in my house. I am aware that no one has a tap on my movement currently. You as well as Obodom are the susceptible targets that must be kept out of danger. You can go in advance to my house. I know that I will be able to track Obodom down and have him also in my house in the next one hour."

Nasser waited for him to decide. Ibifubara is not the type that takes unguided decision. He was therefore giving him the opportunity to scrutinize his suggestion to see how well it suits his investigative and curious mind.

"I will be in your house by 18:50 hours. I leave you to arrange how Obodom will be there before me. Whatever else that has to be decided would be there at the meeting after we must have heard of his meeting at the Presidential Villa. See you then."

Something made him realize that Ibifubara's reason for wanting Obodom seated before his arrival was only to investigate if Nasser has fallen under the monitoring radar of the security men of the presidency. He wanted to ask him but decided to let things be. The remaining that he has to accomplish for the day was to have Obodom in his house before 18:50 hours in the evening.

Before then, he also has to brief him on further developments regarding the Osayiwmense and his mother. Just as there were things for the three of them to decide regarding Obodom's exposure to the political gladiators of the nation, there were also things that he has to decide exclusively by himself in order to chart a way forward. The latest investigation on the health status of Osayiwmense's mother revealed that her mental health was very much unperturbed. She was just suffering from acute shock which resulted from untold violent exposure. What that was could not be decided. The shock in itself has resulted to acute amnesia. First, he has to see Obodom.

Obodom was at home this time around on his arrival.

"I don't know the difference between you and these politicians anymore," he was telling him as he opened the door to grant him access.

"Meaning what? He asked him not fully appreciating his line of thought in saying that. "Do you know me as a member of any political party?" He further enquired of him.

"Not that I know. Your interview today on the television however portrayed you as one."

Obodom was startled into alertness.

"What interview? Do you mean that my interview is already on air? That was very fast of him if so or are you talking of something else?"

"It is the same interview that I am talking of. It is the same interview that you had with Ibifubara that I am referring to. It is a master piece and Ibifubara agrees with me on that. He informed me that he was scared the suddenness of it was going to affect the outcome adversely and was surprised too at your performance."

"That means then that you have seen him? How on earth was he able to know I was going to be there? I have never been taken aback as I was when I saw him. He was the last person I was ever expecting to see. First I did not have enough time to reach out to either you or him and there he turned up like a spirit from the spiritual realm."

"He explained all that when I met him. I was forced to look for him when I saw you on air much to my surprise. It was after I saw the note you left me not too long from when you went with the security men that I first went to look for him but he was not at home. You can imagine then how surprising it was for me to see you on air with same Ibifubara that I could not see to alert him that you had been taken away interview you. He explained that he had pre knowledge of the intention of the security men to come for you.

"In any case you have to come to my house for a meeting of the three of us. The obvious question of what happened we will save so that you don't have to repeat the story the second time. Ibifubara will be in my house by 18:50 hours and he is expecting that you would have been seated before his arrival. If you don't mind, I suggest we go immediately. We have a lot more to discuss afterwards concerning Osayiwmense and the mother. It is nothing to worry about only that there are a whole lot of things to plan and decide together."

Obodom was curious to know about Osayiwmense and his mother however he restrained himself. His attachment to both of them has witnessed dramatic increase over time. They had become members of his family and he loved and cherished them greatly.

Osayiwmense was then a student enrolled formerly in a school. Arrangement was also made for a private lesson to enable him learn better and faster. Obodom was so emotionally moved the day he had some discussions with him. Many things are becoming clearer to him now unlike when he was left solely under the care of his mother. On every occasion they were together there was always that apprehension by Obodom in expectation of numerous questions from him. He was like a soul on an inquest in attempt to discover things that no one had explained to him previously.

"Please be my father" he had pleaded with Obodom in an instance they were together. "It appears I am the only one that had no father in my class. I will want you to be my father." He reemphasized that again to the consternation of Obodom who realized the depth of the yearning in the boy's heart. He realized that he has not fully appreciated parenting for what it actually was. Much as he loved the idea of Osayiwmense desiring him to be his father, he worried that he may become emotionally disturbed if the suspicion people had that he was the product of the violation of his mother by a security guard turns out to be true. Who knows, he may want to claim him later as a son. When and if that eventually happened, he wondered what his countenance would be. Whatever was the case, he vowed to love and provide for him.

"I have heard you Osayiwmense. I will do everything I can to be a good father to you. By the time your mother recovers fully, she would also give you all her love. You really do not have to worry." Silently he prayed that she would actually recover. Every child deserves the guidance of the two parents. It affords the child a balanced development. He wondered again what it was that Nasser wanted to discuss about him and his mother.

FOURTEEN

· ·

It was 18:30 hours when they arrived at Nasser's home. Something immediately struck him as they awaited the arrival of Ibifubara. Since the day that Osayiwmense pleaded with him to be his father he has never been at rest. It was not that he did not like the idea of being his foster father. It was rather the need for him to ensure that he never lacked anything that he could afford. 'It is my divine responsibility that you are properly nurtured into adulthood.' He made that resolution and was determined to do everything possible to guaranty that.

All those worries came afresh again then that he had to be careful in all that he was doing and had to do. 'What would happen to him if anything happens to me?' he asked no one in particular. He was fully aware that the meeting they intended at Nasser's house was not planned without recourse to secrecy from the Presidential Villa security personnel.

"Nasser," he called out at his friend and lawyer, "I want you to prepare a will for me. With all that is happening, it will be foolhardy to assume all is well. I want all that I have willed to Osayiwmense Nigeria. Please I want this to be taken up immediately. Please consider this as important and urgent. In fact I am recording my voice even as we are having this discussion, whatever happens consider it on the bases of my voice instruction that I have authenticated the will. If the hard document is appropriately made ready, I will endorse it but before that happens I have willed everything to him. Until he comes of age, it would be administered in the first instance to have him educated to his first degree in the university"

"I heard your request," responded Nasser, "what brought about the sudden sense of urgency? Did anything transpire between you and these security officers that brought about this sense of urgency?"

"There is nothing that I am really conscious of per say. May be all these need to be careful may have made it paramount to me. If I may say however, I think it has to do with my discussion with Osayiwmense on one hand and my desire that nothing including my death should change or affect his progress in life. I have indeed sent my voice instruction to you on the account of this our discussion.

"I just remembered how he solicited that I be his father. How can you take such a request? So for me it is something really solemn. I earnestly look forward to having him grow up without any further challenge because his biological father is not there for him or because of the condition of his mother."

"May be I have to let you know now that you have brought up the matter. His mother had been discovered free of any mental abnormality. Her case was just that of amnesia. At least let that worry be off your mind. The outstanding concern currently is how to resolve that acute amnesia and Osayiwmense would have the company of his mother in perfect health."

"That is the best news I have heard in recent times," Obodom rejoiced.

It was then that Ibifubara's was heard knocking on the door and Nasser went to bring him in. Immediately they had all exchanged pleasantries the much expected question came.

"Why did they want you so urgently that they had to come to carry you again by themselves?" asked Ibifubara.

"You really gave me the shock of my life. First you got me all so worked up worrying that I was not able to let you know beforehand that I was required at Presidential Villa and then you just appeared like a ghost from nowhere." Obodom enthused before he continued.

"I really do not know what these people are up to. I wish someone can help me find out. Imagine proposing that I head a committee that they want to set up?"

They both turned to look at him in surprise.

"A committee," retorted Nasser. "Wonders shall never end."

"The president wants to set up a governmental committee to investigate the immediate and remote cause of youth restiveness and thinks I am the best qualified to head the committee. I am however bordered. What is the motive of such an offer? Is the president actually concerned about anything or anybody in this country? If really government is concerned why allow things degenerate so badly? What exactly are they up to? I still look at the entire thing as a set up for an ulterior motive.

"So by all outward indication I have stated why I was urgently required at the Presidential Villa."

There was complete silence as they all were in deep thought. It actually made no tangible meaning to anyone them why so much energy was spent looking for Obodom if that was all to it.

"What next do I do, continue to hide in my rat hole as a criminal?" he asked breaking the silence.

"I still maintain my stand that you have to exercise caution. In fact there is more reason to be cautious than ever," Ibifubara stated emphatically. "What was just done may well just be to throw you off guard. If care is not taken you would not even know when you are hit. This people are dangerous. I can bluntly tell you that they have licence to do and undo and nothing will happen. I am not saying that I know exactly what could happen but don't lose your guard."

Obodom could not help thinking that Ibifubara is a natural pessimist. 'If one keeps constant company with him, he will get to the stage of being afraid of his own shadow.'

"I have heard you. I will rather we focus on what can be done to achieve our goal of getting this country better for all of us. I honestly do not like living under fear. It limits me no matter how real they may be." He was constrained to speak out. He was getting terrified all the more and almost developing that consciousness that all those security personnel do was just to kill and he was aware that such mind set was not very healthy for anyone particularly himself.

There were further discussions on the inauguration of the new students' union leadership, how it was going to be covered by a journalist and the direction of speech Obodom was expected to follow. They were rather agreed that the key mandate of theirs was to breed youths that were independent minded and ready to challenge the powers that be to performance. Eventually they dispersed to their individual houses.

Before Obodom left, he requested an appointment with Nasser. There were quite a lot that they had to discuss. There was also the matter of preparing a will that they required to conclude on. 'Even if things may not be as dangerous as Ibifubara portends them to be there was still the need to be prepared for the worst that could happen. A man should not allow his noble plans to be truncated not even by death if he could help.' He thought to himself as he finally bid Nasser farewell.

Consciously he took his mind off the issues of the Presidential villa security personnel to Osayiwmense and his mother. Nasser's information on her development resounded in his mind. 'May be I have to let you know now that you have brought up the matter. His mother had been discovered free of any mental abnormality. Her case was just that of amnesia. At least let that worry be off your mind. The outstanding concern currently is how to resolve that acute amnesia and Osayiwmense would have the company of his mother in perfect health.'

He wondered the story that had been stored up in her mind. From the Doctor's explanation such deep rooted amnesia often resulted from traumatic experiences. 'Who knows the great story that was,' he wondered yet again and again. There was so much joy in his heart that her situation was developing into such a fruitful situation. He could not help remembering that faithful day of his first encounter with them. It was Osayiwmense that first attracted his attention before he realized she was the mother. There was so much joy that his charitable action has impacted on some persons lives.

Whenever such thoughts dwelt in his mind, it dawns on him how much more those that have been elected into political leadership positions can achieve. If only they know how much they can impact on the lives of the ordinary citizens of this country. A lot of the evil that are prevalent in the country would not have been there in the first instance with good governance present.

"How is it they are not aware of this?" he asked no one in particular. Indeed if they are conscious of that no one would have been after him because he spoke to some students to get involved in deciding their future. He would not have had any need to talk to them have the political leadership been up to their responsibility. Instead of facing the demands of governance resources were being deployed wastefully to follow an innocent citizen that had committed no crime. His fear of any dangers that may befall him was suddenly replaced with the zeal to do more.

'Whatever I can do to change the story, I will do. They may come after me; I may indeed be killed, but I will never give up. Let them send legions of soldiers and security personnel after me, I will never give up.' He resolved as he held the pendant on his neck in memory of his late mother. 'For your sake I will continue to fight the course of the down trodden in the society. For your sake, I will fight to ensure that any government of the day will live up to their responsibility. Yes my dear mother, I know that if it was possible for you to see me you will be pleased by my actions.' These were the last thoughts on his mind before he slid off into sleep.

He woke up quite refreshed and happy. The news of Osayiwmense's mother was really the tonic he needed and not all those nonsensical security concerns. He wasted no time in getting ready for his appointment with Nasser. Apart from the documentation aspect of their meeting they were equally to visit her in the hospital. It had been arranged that Osayiwmense would go with them.

There had been a great improvement on her condition. She discusses freely occasionally before the snag in her memory when she relapses into that effort to link her present with the past. She had become conscious of it that there were things she was unable to recollect. She even made the comment that Osayiwmense's name sounded strange to her. This obviously depicts the fact that the name does not conform to whatever tribal language she was used to. That notwithstanding, she had learnt to call him by the name. There had been occasions she made direct enquiry from the Doctor.

"There seems to be flashes of memory that I cannot particularly understand. I kind of think there is something I am supposed to know but somehow, it eludes me when it appears I am just about recollecting it. What am I supposed to do?"

"I am happy you made me aware of this," explained the doctor to her. "You are supposed to do nothing. As a matter of fact you are just to relax and let it come by itself. There had been a lot of improvement in your situation. Don't tense up yourself now. That would not be good for your condition. The more effort you make consciously, the more difficult it gets. It's like the breaking of the day and falling of the night. When it is night it naturally gets dark. When also its day, the day breaks by itself. I want you not to think about it at all."

Her lifestyle has become normal in all ramifications. There was nothing remarkably different between her and any other person. She has also come to know her benefactor and was aware that she does not know him previously. If she did know him, she realized that there must be some inkling to at least alert her to that reality. There was certainty in her mind what a kind man that he was to have come to her help and that of her son Osayiwmense. 'May the almighty God bless him,' she thought.

The Doctor had given his advice that she should not stress herself up to remember things. Try as she did she still found herself unconsciously doing so. There are some vague memories she really would want to put a meaning to. There were also memories of some personalities that she would think meant so much in her life. What really they meant to her and who they were she could not actually comprehend. If only she could put all that together, she would be in a position to know and tell her story.

The most agonising of her puzzles was how she got to the street. 'Where was I before then? What actually made her to leave wherever she came from? Were there no ones that knew who she was and did it not matter to them what happened to her? Would I have lived the rest of my life on the road if Obodom had not come to my rescue?' She struggled with these thoughts until she started having some headache. She had no choice but to adhere to the Doctor's instruction momentarily.

It was at that nick of time that she saw him coming. She was so grateful seeing him coming with her son. Osayiwmense was so happy in his company. He always was anytime they were together. He was of great influence in his life. He loved him so very much. The two looked simply inseparable. What would have happened to him if they have not encountered him? She was so moved that she started praying for God to bless him without measure. What a world there would have been if people like him abound. The life would have worth more for living.

What marvelled her mostly was the fact that he did not know who she was. If he could go that length to render such assistance to a stranger without expecting any reward at all he obviously was naturally a very kind person. Such people are not easy to come by.

The meeting and discussion with the Doctor was very eventful. The Doctor also confirmed to Obodom that Osayiwmense's mother was apart from just recollecting her memory has fully recovered.

"It would be necessary to allow and let her live a normal life by mixing up with other people and also going to places. Chances are that there might be an opportunity to relieve the experience that caused the loss of memory in the first instance." He encouraged him further that there was no need for her to spend much time in the hospital which would have a negative effect on her that something was still wrong with her. She could if he felt there was the need in the future, come for occasional check-up. This would afford the opportunity to check her progress and let her know and feel as any other normal person should. They were all extremely happy as she was finally discharged from the hospital.

FIFTEEN

• •

Mubo has come to become personal friend to Obodom Agozie. Their lives revolved on the same principle of helping out others and proffering solutions and not just complaining. If there was anything that made her to admire him it was the fact that his life was like a service to humanity. Her affection became the more when she got to know of Osayiwmense and his mother. She has also been following up with her development and she was really pleased of her recovery. When therefore she invited Obodom for the inauguration of the new students' union executives she insisted that he was to come with Osayiwmense and his mother. When Obodom wanted to object, she disagreed with him based on the doctor's recommendation that she should lead a normal life as others.

Obodom did not have much impetus to resist their involvement as Mubo had even become closer to the two of them. She had on numerous occasions visited and took them out. The bonding between them had become such that he ceased bordering himself whenever they are together. There were therefore a lot that he did not know about the extent of their friendship and would only realize on the arena in the event of the inauguration.

The event was well publicised and therefore the expectations were rife. Other than the students themselves people of different shades in the society were also interested and came for the event. Obodom has become also a well-known personality in most realms of things in the nation. The earlier event of the manifesto night and the subsequent interview on the television had a more serious effect than Nasser and Ibifubara had expected.

He has been the only one perhaps who has failed to realize he has ceased being an ordinary person. While therefore others are making the effort to put him where he rightly belonged, he made every effort to counter their efforts. However, they were all very determined to solve their problems once and for all. Nature did play its own role too. The scripts of nature's own dramas are written by no other one but nature itself. Every event once the time is right evolved in an unmistaken one direction, just its own manifestation.

The involved characters never ever realize when drums of her music are drawn out. The symphonies of its music are extremely infectious and spontaneous that the dancers are assuredly but yet unconsciously blended into the dance steps that they can't ever recall when they learnt. As their dances proceed, the spectators all marvel. 'They must have learnt the music and danced it from their birth,' they applauded because the music and the dance had become mystic of their existence.

The day and event was set and was bound to commence. From the students to the journalists and unknown to the organizers some security officers drafted from the Presidential Villa were all present. Also unknown to the organizers and even the security operatives, the opposition political party, Freedom Assurance Party, FAP was also observing the emergence of Obodom to limelight. The party had been hopeful that as the main opposition party they will one day successfully dislodge the ruling party from office.

His emergence however has a divisive effect on the party. A group within the party were of the view that Obodom could be co-opted as a member of the party. In their view that will enhance the prospects of the party. It would ensure a better standing for them in the political dispensation of the country. Their view in actual sense is the most logical thing. The other party however had a contrary opinion. The opinion was borne more out of self-preservation. Constituting this group is majorly the main influential members of the party. Their opposition of his involvement in their party is majorly derived from fear of losing their influence and control. Once he joins the party they would be relegated to the background and that they would never want to happen. They had invested so much in the party and vehemently hated some other one currying the control of their party.

The two group were nonetheless united on the need to monitor developments and ultimately be well guided in whatever decision that had to follow. The party had sent some representative to also monitor the events and bring feedback on what had transpired. The instruction to their monitors was definite and that they need not wait for the entire event to be concluded. As Mubo and the entire students' union made frantic effort to have a successful event, other parties also pursued their divergent interests.

The emphasis of the event deliberately was tilted more to promote a new tide of consciousness. This new tide was coincidentally metamorphosed by three persons who for altruistic reasons decided to champion the course. There was a fourth person who had become the arrow of their effort. He was the key figure of all their effort but was not part of their plan.

After Obodom's discussion with Mubo encouraging her to get involved in the events of the nation, she herself gave it the thought that it deserved and was convinced that it was a worthy cause to live and die for. She was well aware that it was not something she could do alone and looked for partners that would help forge a new tide of government. The first person she had a discussion with on the matter was Nasser who had become a bosom friend of Obodom. Nasser on his part co-opted Ibifubara and so was the plan hatched to project Obodom to take over the leadership of the nation.

They were well aware that it may not be an immediate thing to achieve but also agreed that it was a cause that required some urgency. There was the initial confusion of whether to let him know or not. Nasser succinctly made it clear to them that it was better to let situations trap him to take the position they want him to assume. By the time situations and circumstances have made it manifest to him that he had to deliver his nation they would then advise him to take up the challenge also assuring him that he had all their support. The inauguration event had become the launching pad of their plan. Every arrangement that was required to make it a successful one had been made.

Immediately the time came the gladiator of the event Mubo Awoyemi mounted the rostrum. As usual she blended into the situation as if she had prepared for it for decades. She was naturally an organizer that understands what putting an event together meant. Even as her tenure of leadership was coming to an end, the love the students had for her had not waned in anyway. Characteristically and graciously, she looked around as if she was individually acknowledging the presence of every one. There was a dignified calmness everywhere before she began to speak.

"My fellow students and our dignified guests, I welcome you to this great occasion. I must confess that I cherish your love and support in all that I am involved in. I have much to tell you but time will definitely not allow me. I will therefore plead that you excuse my just making a very brief remark to kick off the event." She paused and took her gracious look on everybody once again before she recommenced.

"Does anyone here know Obodom Agozie?" She asked intentionally to wake up their appetite and stare up their expectations. "The first time he was in our mist, we never knew the honour we were done to have him in our mist. It was by popular demand that he has to come again for our inauguration. Let us however get one thing clear. He has always made himself available at our beck and call not because he had so much time but out of his love for the youth and for us. Without much Ado, I have two persons who would introduce Obodom to us because we do not really know him. I will bring him on stage after they have spoken" With a wave of hand to signal some people a beautifully dressed lady and a young boy of about 8 years came up the podium.

The microphone was handed to the lady but the boy demanded to speak first and she gave it to him.

"Good afternoon to everyone that has come here. I know that I look great today without anybody telling me. I am Osayiwmense Nigeria. I want to introduce to you my father who is the reason why I am happy today. I had no father until he became one to me; I never had a name, until he gave me one; I had no home until he gave me one. He is no other person than Obodom Agozie." He introduced as the lady collected the microphone from him.

She took quite a while to put herself together, not used to speaking to a large audience, before she started to speak.

"Good afternoon to you all here present. Please pardon me because I am really scared having to speak to so many of you. I requested for this opportunity from your outgoing president, Mubo Awoyemi and I am grateful to her that she gave me this opportunity.

"It is not long I was discharged from the hospital. As I stand before you, I am still struggling to remember who I am, so don't even ask after my name. I am suffering from amnesia which I am unable to state the cause. The boy that had just spoken is my son. Before now he has no name because I did not give him any. My medical situation almost meant that I was virtually mad and cannot even recall the circumstances of his birth. I requested for this opportunity to show how grateful I am to Obodom. He was not aware I wanted to speak here. I made Mubo promise me not to let him know because I was sure he would not have let me. I want you all to help me appreciate him and pray that God will keep protecting and blessing him."

As she ended, Mubo clasped her into a warm embrace before addressing the audience once again.

"Great students of the nation's greatest institution," she greeted once more.

"Great," chorused the students.

"I want to plead your pardon, if I would affect the quality of Obodom's presentation today. At a great risk of incurring his displeasure I permitted the earlier introduction by Osayiwmense and his mother and he is obviously not pleased with me. I have apologized as much as I can but the upset has taken its toll on him already.

"We are all here for the inauguration of a new students' leadership. Leadership is nothing but service. I took the risk of offending our guest speaker by allowing these two persons to speak. The story of what leadership is must be told in practical terms, which is why I allowed what I did. He understands what leadership is although he shies away from it. Yes leadership is service to the led. The situation and condition of the people that are led must be seen to improve by a conscientious leadership. His life pattern and philanthropy is a lesson in leadership. Please join me in welcoming on stage Obodom Agozie."

The ovation was tumultuous as Obodom proceeded to the stage making effort as he did to wave off from his mind the upset of allowing Osayiwmense and his mother come up the stage. He felt discomfited primarily because he believed works of charity should not be publicized. They should not be for personal aggrandizement. To that extent, he never intended any good he was doing for the purpose of portraying his goodness but from the point of necessity that it was the right thing to do.

"Good afternoon to you all my great friends. I feel subdued from what transpired just now. It is difficult for me to expressly make my point now that I am riding on the cheap publicity of what you heard from my family members. If you permit me however to state a fact, it is that what you have heard from them should not prey you sense of judgement to scrutinize all that I have to say. Challenge my assertions from the point of what it should be and not from the weak point of emotions.

"I do not also want anyone to assume that I am running down the establishment as a proof of my credibility or integrity. All that I am saying is that we all have to improve our situation and that starts from improving ourselves. The quality of the people we are is what determines the quality of the nation that we have. It is therefore necessary that we start from auditing ourselves and find out if the quality of the persons we are suits the quality of people we want to pilot our affairs.

"We have all gathered here for the inauguration of the new students' union leadership. As we ponder on that we also have to reflect on the leadership of our nation. It all begins from here. I have seen your bond with your outgoing executives. Why was there such a great bond between the students and their leadership? It is also relevant that the incoming leadership be keen on finding out the correct answer to this question. The next relevant question to the discus will be what kind of leadership do you; the incoming leadership want to offer? Let also the student body ask themselves what kind of leadership are they expecting?

"The reason I demanded that these questions be asked is that it provides check and balances in the delivery of service by the leadership and demand pressure from the students that the right thing be done. Once the leadership are sure of the reason for the offering of their leadership and are also aware of the expectation of the students, it dawns on them that there is no chance for excuses. It keeps them on their toes to be creative in proffering solutions to the ever increasing challenges facing the students generally.

"Now reflecting on our nation vis-à-vis leadership as I have propounded for the incoming leadership and the students themselves, I want to state that we have a failing system that requires an urgent solution. We have a need to redeem our nation and my interest and demand is that the youths of this nation must wake up. We have trusted the system but we have also failed as individuals; we have failed to challenge our leaders to deliver. We have not realized the relevance of making our demands and challenging the system to perform or quit the stable of leadership. This is essentially why I have declared that it starts from here.

"Like I asked what you expect of your incoming leadership, I also ask you, what is your expectation on the leadership of the nation? It is not enough for us to relax and be satisfied with whatever they are willing to give us. Time has come for us to articulate our needs and requirements and insist that the leadership we have must meet those needs and demands of ours. That is the area of our failing.

"As I commend your outgoing leadership on what they were able to achieve for the good of you all, I challenge the incoming one to realize that if they fail to achieve what their predecessor were able to accomplish they should realize that it is failure in itself. I also do not advocate that your outgoing should go into oblivion and think that their job is done. I want to tell them that the work had just commenced. They have to not only advise the current leadership but also get ready to advance into the realm of the national leadership in whatever manner and form they can. The journey of rescuing this nation has commenced and I ask, 'who is coming along with me?' Thank You."

The ovation was tumultuous as he set to leave the stage. The students kept clapping and yelling in appreciation. What happened afterwards was spontaneous and unexpected. A student had jumped the protocol and sprang to the stage with a placard with the inscription, **OBODOM FOR PRESIDENT – OUR COUNTRY NEEDS YOU NOW.**

"Yes oooh!" The audience shouted in the affirmative to the inscription on the placard. A couple more from among the audience came up stage trying to carry Obodom shoulder high. The organizers and the campus security had to rally immediately to clear the stage and calm the situation.

Immediately after his speech and his ascent from the rostrum arrangements were concluded for Obodom to depart without the knowledge of the general students. All other things that remained of the event were exclusively for the students and there were actually no reason for him to stay further. It was indeed a successful event by any measure. Mubo was very elated at the performance of Obodom as regarded the new tide of governance consciousness. She was quite sure also that both Nasser and Ibifubara would be excited by the time they watched the clip of all that happened.

It was actually Ibifubara that came up with the idea of Osayiwmense and his mother being the ones that would introduce Obodom. To him, that would be the greatest selling point of the event. Both the media world and the entire nation would marvel at the character of the man who the youths would want to lead the nation. They would be forced to evaluate him in real terms and would have no choice but to agree with the youths that a candidate befitting to be the president of the nation has been found.

He also delegated a crew of three journalists who were supposed to ensure effective coverage of the programme. Later their individual coverage would be evaluated and the most apt edition would be adopted for telecast to the public to give the desired effect and message. His expectations were that it would be a master piece.

Mubo had detailed security for the event on need to escort Obodom and the family out of the arena. She went with them the extent she could and returned to join the ceremony. She felt fulfilled at the success that had been achieved and was hopeful that ultimately the nation would get the leader it deserved for the progress and happiness of all.

SIXTEEN

• •

"Look," shouted Osayiwmense pointing at a man that was running frantically. From all indications he appeared to be running to mingle with the crowd. A man was running after him with a gun held out. Then the staccato sounds of gun shots shot at him by a man pursuing him.

"Oh!' Shouted Osayiwmense's mother in anguish and fell to her face.

All that were around her turned to see what happened to her not excluding Obodom and Osayiwmense. Their initial fear was that she could have been hit by a stray bullet. Nothing on her however suggested that. She simply lied on the floor. Fortunately they were still within the vicinity of the university so she was immediately taken to the University's Teaching Hospital where she was being treated previously.

She was moved into the emergency ward. Her medical file was retrieved and from the entries, Dr John Isikwe who had been handling her case was called up. Before his arrival however she had recovered her consciousness but was crying.

Suddenly the memory that had eluded her kept flashing back.

"I now remember, I now remember that I am Deborah Okolie. I do remember the horrific incident that befell my community in general and my husband, Kenneth Ofili Okolie in particular. It had all happened in my home town of Asaba on the 7th of October 1967. That was the day my husband was shot dead among his fellow kinsmen in an open square at Ogbe-Osawa village of Asaba. We had just married and I was about 3 months pregnant. It was so devastating losing such a loving husband. That day my world came to an end." She started crying uncontrollably.

The Doctor was very happy at the development and sent a nurse to call in Obodom. He rushed in with Osayiwmense immediately he heard about the development. Just as the Doctor had told them after his initial diagnosis, recovery from amnesia is often triggered off by the recurrence of any similar case to the one that traumatized the patient into it in the first instance.

"Well, the tide of the day has actually brought you good fortune. I recommend you go home, allow her a lot of rest. She may relieve the trauma once in a while until she is fully relieved. Let no one pressure her for any story other than however she wants to tell it herself."

She was finally discharged and they set to go home. The event of the day was however yet to be over. As they made to come out of the hospital premises, a motor bike came very close to where they were, the rider came almost to a stop and his passenger pulled a gun aimed at Obodom's heart and shot twice and the bike sped off again. Osayiwmense was able to identify that it was the same man who was being chased and shot at. The bike had actually been in wait to take him on course to assassinate Obodom. Instructions had been given by the sponsors on hearing about his speech and all that transpired that he must not live. In the cause of their mission they had been spotted by the men dispatched from Presidential Villa whose own mission was not to kill but to affect arrest. A more opportune time was being planned when they discovered the assassin's plot. Unfortunately they could not be stopped from taking the shots at their target.

The journey home was truncated by the sad incident. An ambulance was brought to the scene. As they made effort to put his body on the stretcher, he turned to Osayiwmense smiled at him and in his gasping breadth said,

"My son, you remember you once asked me to be your father. I have accepted. Your mother will look after you. I will not, not die. I will." he lost all consciousness as they finally put his body into the ambulance with Osayiwmense and his mother Deborah wailing in anguish as the man they had grown to love was driven back into the hospital not knowing whether he would ever survive those bullets that were shot at him.